Among
Animals 3

Among Animals 3

*The Lives of Animals and Humans in
Contemporary Short Fiction*

Ashland
Creek
Press

Among Animals 3: The Lives of Animals and Humans in
Contemporary Short Fiction
Edited by John Yunker

Published by Ashland Creek Press
Ashland, Oregon
www.ashlandcreekpress.com

Library of Congress Cataloging-in-Publication Data

Names: Yunker, John, editor.
Title: Among animals 3 : the lives of animals and humans in contemporary
short fiction / edited by John Yunker.
Description: Ashland, Oregon : Ashland Creek Press, [2022] | Series: Among
animals ; vol 3
Identifiers: LCCN 2021050585 (print) | LCCN 2021050586 (ebook) | ISBN
9781618221001 (paperback) | ISBN 9781618221018 (hardcover) | ISBN
9781618221025 (ebook)
Subjects: LCSH: Human-animal relationships--Fiction. | Animals--Fiction. |
LCGFT: Short stories.
Classification: LCC PN6071.A7 A48 2022 (print) | LCC PN6071.A7 (ebook) |
DDC 808.8/0362--dc23/eng/20211105
LC record available at https://lccn.loc.gov/2021050585
LC ebook record available at https://lccn.loc.gov/2021050586

Contents

Introduction

Animals speak. But humans are, with few exceptions, ill-equipped to understand them.

Fortunately, we have writers.

Writers play the critical role of interpreter, positioned between humans and the billions of nonhuman animals with whom we share this planet. In *Among Animals 3*, you will meet some of these writers as well as the animals who inspire them. Some of these stories are as challenging as others are inspiring, and we hope you come away from them feeling as enlightened as we felt upon first reading them.

While these stories are fiction, their messages feel all too real, all too relevant. Perhaps it is because fiction breaks down the walls that we have long built up between humans and animals.

We began the *Among Animals* series to showcase the power that fiction can bring to issues for which facts and data too often fall flat. As with climate change. Or animal protection. Or the ever-present myth that animals are on this planet as our subordinates. Carol J. Adams once wrote, "You can't argue with mythology." But fiction can challenge mythology in ways that mere facts cannot. Fiction deploys passions and emotions and dreams to disrupt time-worn habits and traditions. Fiction can change the world.

A collection for the Anthropocene

With this edition, we discovered stories that, as a whole, feel more visceral, more urgent than ever. Perhaps it is climate change and the plight of animal species around the globe that compels us all, writers and readers alike, to take a closer look at what we are so close to losing. Perhaps it is also the plight of the human species and the many stresses of a tiny virus. The rapid spread of Covid has underscored that we humans are not just animals but highly social animals who can spread a virus faster than any other species on this planet. And perhaps because of Covid, we face the simple realization that life is short and we must make the most of our time and our talents.

Fortunately, these writers have made the most of their talents in writing about animals, about species ranging from dogs and cats to chickens and pigs. In one story, we meet a donkey. In another, a jaguar. And we even encounter a species or two not yet formally identified.

Seeing through the eyes of animals

The animal perspective is perhaps the most challenging perspective to write, as we are all guessing in the end. And yet we can imagine what an animal might be thinking or feeling, and this simple act, the act of empathy, is fundamental to awakening humanity to the challenges that animals face. In "Separation," Janay Brun blends the journeys of migrants and a jaguar along the American border; in doing so, she underscores the painful truths of suffering among human and nonhuman animals. In "Liftoff," Ingrid L. Taylor takes us inside a primate's body as he is sent into space, never to return.

Jacquie Vervain, in "Behind the Chokecherry," goes one step further, imagining the journey of a pig in the afterlife, a haunting story that blends religion and ritual with the plight of a heartbreakingly beautiful pig.

Relationships, human and other
In "The Art of Dying," Nadja Lubiw-Hazard shares a passionate tale of love as a rescued crow returns with gifts of gratitude for a woman with a failing body part, not her own.

Kipp Wessel, in "Brasita de Fuego," writes about a vermilion flycatcher found far outside of his range and a narrator who is also a bit lost and soon to be found. Diane Lefer, in "Survival Skills," shares a uniquely Southern Californian tale of humans and mountain lions and what happens when their worlds quite literally collide.

Perspectives on a virus
The pandemic is represented in this collection as well. JoeAnn Hart examines the intersection of Covid with our neighborhood corvids in her touching story "Flying Home." And in "Ava," Denise Rettew takes us into a child's world where the truth is not clouded by rationalizations or other adult "realities" but where reality and magic blur together.

Exploring the world of the animal activist
What does it mean to be an animal activist? The word *activist* is often loaded with baggage for those whose livelihoods are threatened by humans standing up for animals. Yet we are all animal activists in our own ways. You don't have to look far in life to find someone who has adopted an animal from a shelter or fed a stray. As more people become aware of the plight of animals around them, they are changing their behaviors (adopting instead of buying, supporting local animal sanctuaries, giving up meat and dairy) as well as speaking up, writing letters, attending city council meetings, holding signs in protest.

The stories "For the Animals" by Setter Brindle Birch and "The Pet Project" by Helia S. Rethmann take us inside the worlds of animal activism and protection, worlds that present unique challenges all their own.

Looking backward

As in previous editions of *Among Animals*, we continue to look back at our history, but not in reverence for the ways we coexisted with animals. The word *coexist* is too liberally used even today. In J. Bowers's story "One Trick Pony," we witness the cruelty that Hollywood has inflicted on animals ever since its beginnings, in this fictional version of a tragic and true story of a horse who resisted. In "The Ass of Otranto" by Marilyn Moriarty, we go back in time through the eyes of one such defendant, found guilty of murder.

Looking forward

You will also find stories here that gaze into the speculative future. In "Last of the Sasquatch Wilds," James Edward O'Brien imagines the future of a purported species that actually looks painfully familiar today, with other endangered species. And "The Curious Case of the Cave Salamander" by Gwen C. Katz takes urban myths to a darkly humorous extreme; as the character Kira says, "humans had a good run."

Writers make us look

In "Everything That Can Go Wrong with a Body," Elisabeth Benjamin presents us with the violent business of a small chicken farm through the eyes of a narrator who cannot bring herself to witness the act of killing. By the end of the story, she is compelled to watch, as we, the readers, join her. It is not an easy sight to behold.

Perhaps the first great step we all must take in improving the lives of animals—all animals—is not to look away. The second great step we all must take is to act. In "Brothers" by Charlene Logan, a number of people bear witness to dogs in need, but nobody responds in time. Writers challenge us to look and to act.

These stories challenge us to see what we have tried to avoid seeing. It's only by looking straight on—and acting upon what we witness—that we can ensure a better future for animals and the planet.

Thank you for joining us on this journey.

Thank you for not looking away.

— John Yunker

The Art of Dying

Nadja Lubiw-Hazard

She had a scar on her throat, over her trachea, a beautiful puckered vulnerability that I couldn't stop staring at. She was sharp-angled and luminous, like a sickle moon. There was a skinny brindle pit bull lying across her feet, all ribs and muscles and lolling tongue, fur the color of burnt butternut squash. She glanced up and saw me staring; the dog looked up, too, with wide-set, ghostly blue eyes. I looked away and stumbled back, dizzy from all those eyes, as if I were being appraised by a multi-ocular divine being.

When I told her how I felt under the gaze of those four luminous eyes, weeks later, as we lay on a grassy hillock, watching the Perseid meteor shower, she said nothing. But hours later, as we lay entwined in bed, her head resting between my breasts, both of us somewhere between wakefulness and sleep, she whispered, "Like Argus, with a hundred eyes that never sleep." She sighed, and I felt her breath tickle against my naked skin. "Always watching."

"What?" I asked, coming fully awake. "Who's Argus?" But she wouldn't say more. That's what she was like, full of sublime silences and unspoken words, not with any hint of shyness or awkwardness, but in a more profound way: the quiet of a cedar tree, of a pink evening sky, of a wary wolf. For a long time after she left I could still hear her silence, lingering nearby, longing to be heard.

—

Once she spoke for over an hour, the day she told me about the crow. The dog and I both listened with rapt attention, afraid any movement might break the spell of tongues she was under.

She was eleven, she said, living in a basement room with her dad, in a run-down bungalow on a dead-end street. The place belonged to one of her dad's old friends. Maybe they had sold dope together when they were younger, she said, or played together in a grunge band.

"I'd just had surgery, the third, maybe the fourth." She skimmed a finger over the scar on her neck, circled back, and caressed it tenderly. The dog watched her without blinking, his tail swishing back and forth across the floorboards. He couldn't contain himself; his love for her was always spilling over.

Mostly her dad was gone, she told me. Sometimes when he returned he'd bring something for her: a pair of gerbils in a shoebox, faded Levi's from the Goodwill, a couple of tattered paperbacks. One day he brought her Zora Neale Hurston's book *Their Eyes Were Watching God.*

"I was supposed to be doing schoolwork to stay caught up with my fifth grade class. Instead I was lying in a hammock underneath the lilac tree in the backyard, reading. I'd never read a book like that before. It woke me up to the world, to all its heartache and tenderness. And it taught me to be defiant."

She laughed and then stopped abruptly, like the lid on a music box slamming shut.

She continued her story. One morning she found a crow caught in the wooden fence behind the hammock at the back of the yard. The bird's head was wedged in the small gap between two boards; all that was visible was the headless body and wings hanging down, the tail feathers spread out in a little black fan. The crow must have been there for a while, battering his wings up and down against the fence. There were two arcs of blood splattered on the boards, one on his left, one on his right, the exact same distance away from the body. A little shiver ran through her as she spoke, and the dog whined, a high-pitched, rusty squeak. I pictured the bird, held in that terrible embrace, bracketed by his own blood. The macabre symmetry of it seemed beautiful.

"I slid him up and out," she said, "and just held him in my arms. But he wasn't dead. He was blinking! He was still alive!"

I saw the crow's third eyelid flashing white across the blackness of his eye, like a little burst of sheet lightning. She told me about nursing him back to health: massaging his cold claws; bathing the bloodied wings; microwaving one of her dad's sweatshirts and then bundling the bird up in it to warm him up; feeding him scrambled eggs and ketchup, the only meal she knew how to make.

"I fell in love," she said. Wistfully, as if she knew she would never feel that way again. There was a sharp pain in my chest, as if the crow's icy claws had grasped hold of my heart. I heard what she had left unsaid in all of our time together, what I knew she would never say to me.

"He got stronger, and then one day he flew away. He just left." She stopped speaking. In the silence I imagined I could hear the biting lice gnawing through the crow's downy feathers, hear the rustle of tattered wings taking flight, hear his mother's raucous squawks calling him home, calling to him from a thousand miles away.

The dog barked sharply. We both looked at him, and her hand fluttered down to rest on his wide forehead. "Shush," she said. She jumped up and retrieved a battered gray fishing tackle box from under her bed, unclasped the latches, and opened the lid. "Look," she whispered. "Look what the crow brought me."

There were six trays, each filled with multiple compartments, each one containing a single small item. She held up a luminescent yellow marble, striped and swirled like Jupiter. She told me she found it the day after the crow flew away, on her flip-flops, which she had left lying beneath the hammock.

She showed me one thing after another, lifting each one from its holding place: a Christmas pine cone, dusted with gold glitter; a cracked snail shell; a rusted pentacle earring; the shiny reddish-brown exoskeleton of a june bug; a tangle of purple yarn. She had favorites. Most of the time, the gifts appeared when she wasn't there, she said, but one time the crow had landed in the lilac tree above her, jumping nimbly from branch to branch. He had flown down to her and spread his wings out wide, dipped his glossy black head low, and then dropped a heart-shaped metallic tag at her feet. It was a 1998 rabies tag from Val-d'Or, Quebec, tag #1621. She tucked the tag back in its place and then held out two gray stones, one flattish, the other smaller and egg-shaped. She told me how she had watched from the low basement window as the crow placed the flat stone down, then worked with his beak to balance the second stone atop the first. "He made me a sculpture," she said, placing the stones carefully back in the box. "He was a fucking artist." She shook her head, her eyes wide with awe.

I had a surge of jealousy for the crow, the finder of hidden things, an intense envy for the breathless catch in her voice when she talked about his rasping black laughter. It wasn't a new feeling. I was jealous all the time: jealous of the dog, the way he licked the inside of her pale knees with his long wet tongue, the way she rubbed her bony knuckles tenderly across his massive forehead; jealous of her ex-girlfriend Therese, who sent postcards, one of the hot springs in Poços de Caldas, another of the sand dunes and lagoons at Lençóis Maranhenses National Park, signed *all my love*; jealous of the flimsy white bohemian smock with embroidered peacock eyes that she wore, the way it spent the day sliding against her small jutting breasts, so, so intimately.

"Once he brought me a dead baby bird," she said. She pulled out a stack of papers from the bottom of the tackle box. Underneath them I saw a pair of flip-flops and a tattered paperback copy of Zora's book. She showed me the drawings she had done of the corpse. They were crude sketches: the beak a jarring gash of yellow, the closed eye like a blueberry, a bloated abdomen, spindly splayed legs. "I watched it decompose all summer, until it was just a little pile of tiny bones."

I could see them, the bones, in a corner compartment of the tackle box: the smooth dome of the baby bird's skull; the miniscule ribs, curling in on themselves; the fragile femurs; the keel bone, sharp and curved, like a scythe. Her fingers touched down on them, brailling them, reading the gift of death. But she didn't lift them out to show them to me. Instead, she closed the lid of the box and clasped it shut.

—

In the weeks that followed, I was filled with restlessness, with an incredible dissatisfaction for everything about myself. The things that had once made me feel I was special all became obsolete. My wild orange curls suddenly seemed crass, and I walked into Tony's Barber Shop one Tuesday and got them shaved off. My work at the hospital seemed like an overdone plot from half a dozen TV shows. My hockey skates hung in my closet, unused, their once-gleaming blades gathering dust. I had no interest in myself. I disappeared, became a hull that contained only my immense desire for her.

One day I called in sick and followed her around the city. I wasn't even sure what it was she did for a living; I knew only that it had something to do with medieval manuscripts or ancient maps. Her life was like the place marked *here the lions abound*, the uncharted territory, unwilling to be discovered.

I waited across the street from her apartment, lingering with the nannies who were dropping kids off at the public school. My breath caught in my throat when she emerged. Would she see me lurking nearby, watching her? But she walked swiftly away, the brindle dog at her heels.

I followed. She stopped at the Asian grocery, bought a handful of cherries, then walked to the nearby ravine. I watched the dog race ahead down the wooden steps, but I didn't follow; I waited for them to re-emerge, an hour later. She spent the rest of the day sitting at the patio of a vegan café, the dog curled up at her feet, talking with a woman who was wearing a gossamer pink hijab. They seemed intimate. They touched each other easily, ate food from one another's plates, laughed together with their heads thrown back, teeth flashing white in the sun. I watched from across the street as she reached up and gathered her pale hair into a knot at the crown of her head, exposing the Sanskrit tattoo at the nape of her neck, and then let it fall back over her shoulders again. It was a gesture so familiar to me, yet she remained so unknown, that I winced. Rage pulsed through me. I wanted to shake her until she convulsed and split apart, until her insides spilled out, until I could see all that she kept hidden.

When I asked her later about her day, she told me only about walking the dog in the ravine, about what she thought might be a giant hogweed plant she had seen growing near the riverbank, the large umbels of dainty white flowers.

We fought on her birthday a few weeks later, after she refused to tell me where she'd been earlier. I accused her of all her silences: the silence of apathy, the silence of mystery, the silence of neglect. We were in her bedroom. The tackle box sat at the foot of her bed, left there from the day she had shown me the crow's gifts. I snatched it up and shook it furiously. "This isn't love," I screamed, hurling the box against the wall behind her. "You're heartless. You're not even capable of love."

She frowned, little creases between her eyes forming like frost on a window, icy and delicate. The only sound was the faint rustle of her emerald-green swing dress, the one that I had bought for her at a vintage shop on the weekend, as she bent to pick up the overturned box.

"I was at the cardiologist," she said, shaking her head ever so slightly.

"Why?" I shrieked. "Why?"

She shrugged, an elegant lift of her shoulder, like a swan raising her wing to preen. She didn't answer, but it was suddenly clear to me that all her surgeries had been of the heart. *She's dying,* I thought. I fell to my knees, sick with remorse. A moment ago her unknowable silences had seemed monstrous; now it was me who was the monster.

She bent down and opened the lid of the box, then sat, tucking her feet under the wide green swirl of the skirt of the dress. The items had shifted, fallen from their compartments. She picked up a three-holed, pearly white button and tucked it back into its place, lovingly, as if she were placing a fallen baby bird back into a nest. Her cheeks were flushed a soft pink, the same color as the inner pinna of the dog's ears. I didn't speak. When she was done replacing everything, she closed the box and stood. I heard the same rustling sound as her dress shifted, and I imagined the sound of a baby crow, learning to talk, the high whispering trills and soft chortles she might make.

"I have a bioprosthetic heart valve. From a pig. But it's failing me." She touched a hand lightly to her chest. "Sometimes I have dreams. Nightmares, I guess, about the pig, coming to find me. She's not alive, but she's not dead either. She comes for me, asking for her heart back. I always try, in the dream, to give it back. 'Take it!' I scream, and I start clawing at my own chest, trying to rip it out. She watches me. She has the most beautiful eyes, soft and gray."

I pictured the pig's eyes: the pink eyelids, the tiny pale eyelashes, the whites of the eyes shining like two crescent moons.

"They're filled with pity. She pities *me*! I have a piece of her heart, but she … she … " A small, gulping sob escaped her lips. The dog paced in a tight circle around her, whimpering in distress. I did nothing. She was so lovely, in all her brokenness. I wanted to throw back my head and keen; to seize her trembling body and pull it to mine, crushing that shimmering green dress between us; to tear out her treacherous heart and replace it with my own, but I remained still. Perhaps there was a secret cruelty hidden deep inside me that I wasn't even aware of that stopped me from reaching for her. Or maybe I was stilled with pity, just like the pig in her dreams. But in the moment, all that I was aware of was my own inconsequentiality. She radiated like the sun, blazing and burning in front of me, shimmering with her own mortality.

—

I never saw her again, after that night. When I went to her apartment and knocked on her door a few days later, a hollow sound echoed back. I pressed my ear against the door, listening for the dog's nails to click across the floorboards, or for the wet snuffling sound of his nose at the crack below the door. But there was only the silence of absence. I waited for hours. Eventually I slid down the wall across from her apartment door and fell into a fitful sleep, curled up on the cold floor. Her landlord, an ancient, gnarled man with gun-black eyes, kicked me awake, sometime after two in the morning. "She gone," he said. "She take all her things." He looked at me impassively. "Now you go, too."

A week later I received a small package in the mail. There was no note, but I wouldn't have expected one anyway. Inside, wrapped tenderly in pale yellow tissue paper, was a small, slender piece of a femur, fractured off at mid-shaft. It was less than a bone, really, just a little jagged shard of one. It was hollow, made for flight.

For the Animals

Setter Brindle Birch

We've all been there. We know how it is when you're trying to persuade someone and they just won't listen. It's so frustrating. The good news is that you can work on being more persuasive. Arm yourself with facts. Rehearse in front of the mirror. You can also keep our Frequently Asked Questions leaflets on hand and give them out when the occasion calls for it. I'll send you a pack of 200 to get you started—hope it helps!
    For the Animals,
    Moose

—

A few weeks ago I saw my cousin Dev at a family gathering, something I generally prefer to avoid, but it was my grandniece's graduation, and of course I wanted to be there. Dev was there with his wife, his son, and a couple of grandchildren I never knew he had. He's changed a lot since the days when I used to babysit him.

While we were still in the parking lot, he dredged up an

old argument about the animal rights group where I did three internships back in the nineties. Apparently it's in the news again, but I don't follow the news, and I told him that.

"My Anne Boleyn hologram shows are all I need to stay in touch with the world," I said. It was an exaggeration, but only a small one. We walked into the hotel, about twenty minutes from my sister's new place in Halifax, and looked around for the grand ballroom.

The conversation went back and forth like this for a while, and I mentioned that I had not, of course, agreed with *all* the organization's policies.

"I guess I thought I could do more good there than at home," I said. I would have added, if I thought Dev cared, that there hadn't been many choices back then. Other organizations of that era weren't a whole lot better.

"I'm sure there must have been other protest groups," Dev sneered, anticipating my complaint. At seventy-four, he's still a child walking around with underpants on his head.

"Six people with hand-drawn signs," I conceded. "If you want to call that a protest."

Just then my grandnephew, Foal, heard us talking. He's in high school now, and he's a member of his school's antispeciesist advocacy club.

"What did you do there?" he asked me. "Did you, like, go on protests every day?"

He sat down next to me in the fancy hotel lobby where we were all waiting, none of us sure where to go next.

"No, only once in a while," I said. "Usually I worked in the office. Stuffing envelopes, putting together information packs, things like that. For a while I helped out in the library, filing away media clippings. Eventually I settled down in the writing department, answering letters. That was my favorite job."

A holographic elephant passed by, and Dev's grandchildren got up, squealing and trying to pet the gentle being's trunk. Kids that age have trouble distinguishing between the metaverse and real life.

Dev's wife distracted them and took them to the bathroom down the hall.

"What kinds of letters did you get?" Foal asked me.

"Well, there was no metaverse in those days," I said. "The internet was new, and we weren't using email yet. No social media, no augmented reality apps or hologram shows, nothing like that. There was this big stack of papers, and we always seemed to be months behind. Some people wrote really nice letters, saying they supported the work we were doing, and other people wrote nasty letters. Calling us idiots and crazies and terrorists—you know, the usual stuff."

"The usual stuff?" Foal asked. "Like … ?"

"Oh, letters arguing against veganism or defending vivisection, letters telling us we sucked, that sort of thing. We even got a slew of letters accusing us of putting antifreeze in the water troughs at an agricultural fair."

"Seriously?" asked Foal.

"Was it true?" asked Dev.

"It was a made-up story," I said coldly. "There were all sorts of rumors going around back then. Another letter I remember was about some kind of conspiracy. The writer was … oh, she described this elaborate plot against her. There must have been an animal connection in there somewhere, but for the life of me it was … well, it was buried under a lot of crap."

"Imagine that," said Dev, but I paid no attention.

Dev's wife brought the kids back and got them settled in an armchair with a better view of the holograms.

"An employee read it out loud at a staff meeting," I told

Foal after stopping to think about his question. "I remember now. It was an example of the kinds of letters I got, to show how I was helping. They were acknowledging my work, and I appreciated that."

"So what did you tell the conspiracy theory lady?" Foal asked.

I thought about it some more.

"I must have told her to call the police, I guess? I can't remember it very well now, but I had to take it as seriously as any other letter and not even *imply* I thought otherwise."

We all got distracted for a moment when Dev's grandson grabbed his sister's Okja doll and Dev's son had to intervene.

"Macy Starfish was there, too," I recalled after the conflict was resolved, "and she said they were lucky to have me. You know, she was so busy, traveling all over the world meeting with VIPs. I thought it was nice of her to take time to mention my paltry efforts."

Foal was intrigued. "You met Macy Starfish? Really?"

I nodded yes.

"Wow. What did you think of her?"

"A very nice woman," I said. "As far as I knew her, anyway. A very inspiring speaker, too."

"We had a debate about her in our antispeciesist history class last week," Foal said. "She sounded scary. Kind of like that prima donna character from *Okja*."

"That's not the side of her I knew," I said. "I guess we all wear different faces, though, don't we?"

Dev, who was still making faces at us from his end of the sofa, asked the question I knew was coming. "Did you ever have to send out a reply you *didn't* agree with?"

"Of course," I said evenly, refusing to react to his provocation. Naturally, I explained, our correspondence had to reflect an official point of view.

Dev rolled his eyes, and I opened my mouth to say something. That's when my sister came marching down the hall, motioned impatiently toward the seven of us, and ushered us all into the reception hall for the ceremony.

—

In response to your question about the homeless animal problem in your community, I'm sending you our Homeless Animal Information Pack and I hope you will find it helpful. Thanks again for your kind words, and for your interest in helping homeless animals.

For the Animals,
Moose

—

Thinking back to that time in my life, that time in my twenties when I was learning how to be an activist, it's Trudi's face that stands out. Having her jump into bed with me or wag her tail just for me. Seeing her look up at me in the library and knowing she felt safe in my presence.

And our walks—Trudi and I used to walk everywhere together. We walked through a park with deer, we walked through a cemetery, we walked past gaudy religious lawn ornaments. We had some long conversations, and some close calls, too.

Once, we were passing a house near the office when a rottweiler escaped from the backyard and charged out to the street. The rottweiler didn't bite Trudi, but she looked as if she wanted to. A woman in pajamas came out, flustered and apologetic, and brought the big dog inside, but Trudi had already slipped her collar in a panic. She ran ahead of me, and I thought I'd lost her.

"Wait," I said, and she did. Trudi was a strong-willed dachshund, and that's the one and only time she ever listened to me.

Cory used to bring Trudi to work with him almost every day. During my first internship, they were at the intern house most days, too. Even in the quiet season between early October and the end of the year it was nearly full, with six interns from four different countries. It was a beautiful old house on a wooded lot in the Boston suburbs, with two goats in the backyard named Babe and Emma. The organization was getting ready to move across the country, and the goats were among the last residents who still needed homes. The parrot, Sondheim, went to a sanctuary shortly before I left in December.

Soon after I came back for a second stint, plans to relocate the headquarters got underway, and For the Animals donated the house to another organization on the condition that Babe and Emma could stay. Interns left, new interns came to town, and a few of us moved in with Cory. That's how Trudi and I got so close. It's how we started taking walks together.

Our first walk was sometime in February or March. It was the same day as our volunteer trip to the local humane society, just a few days after an awkward conversation in Cory's kitchen.

"Moose, are you pro-euthanasia?" he asked me.

"For people?" I blurted out.

"No," he answered. "For animals in animal shelters."

"Yes, in some cases," I must have said. Or, "It depends on the situation." I was fumbling for words, but I remember spitting out, "Like if the animal is terminally ill or something. Why?"

"They're going to be euthanizing," he said, as if it were self-evident. "Not in front of us, but … "

Cory was rarely at a loss for words, but he seemed to be floundering. His roommate Bob, who was standing there in the kitchen with us, helped him out.

"Do you want to support an organization that kills animals?" Bob asked me.

I wanted to join the trip regardless of the shelter's policies, and that's what I told Cory and Bob. So we all got up early the following Saturday, and Cory drove us to a shabby building downtown with dim lighting.

The shabbiness, he informed us, was the fault of a no-kill group that had briefly taken charge before a counter-revolt set things right.

In the cat room, I asked a kennel worker about the shelter's adoption rates. "A lot of them do get adopted," she said, but the grace period was only five days.

When the cleaning was done, I asked the shelter manager if I could walk dogs.

"I have a rule for dog walkers," she said. "If a dog gets away from you and gets lost, you don't walk another one. Got it?"

I walked a shy Yorkie and a boisterous schnauzer in the cement courtyard behind the building, but then I had to sit down. For the last hour or so I sat in the reception room and waited, watching as people and animals passed by.

Maybe it was all the strange people, or maybe she smelled something on our clothes, but Trudi behaved oddly when we got back. There was a gaggle of us in the living room—Cory, two or three of his colleagues, Bob, a handful of interns.

"She's a nervous dog," said Bob, and later that day I asked Cory if I could walk Trudi for the first time.

"Wear her out," he said.

After that, we'd go out together on my lunch breaks, on weekends, and nearly every day after work.

"She's my stress reducer," I told Cory's other roommate. But when she asked why I was stressed, I couldn't explain it.

That roommate moved out in April after a tearful confrontation with Cory over unpaid rent. Bob left around the same time. There was a turnover of interns, too: By May there were five of us in the house, plus Cory and two new roommates. Two people to a room, Cory in the basement, and one of the more dedicated interns on the living room sofa. Trudi had to vie for attention with three cats and a newly adopted Weimaraner whose stunning good looks drew stares on the street.

One day a suspicious package arrived at the office, and we all had to leave the building. People whispered as they filed out a side door, unsure what was happening or how serious it might be. I tried to convince Trudi to take a walk, but she wouldn't budge from the parking lot.

"She wants to be where the action is," Cory said. He crossed the parking lot, talked to the police for a few minutes, and announced what was in the package.

"Cell phone!"

Cory seemed amused, nonchalant. Someone had mailed the phone in as a donation, apparently with innocent intentions. Time to get back to work.

—

Your love for little Laci comes through in your letter and I can see that you really don't want to give her up. Luckily, these days there are many ways to manage allergies so that humans and their cherished companion animals can stay together. I'm sending you our information pack on Dealing with Animal Allergies—hope it helps!

Also, about Laci's arthritis and itchy skin, there are a number of promising treatments that you might want to explore. The enclosed article about holistic vets may be of some interest.

For the Animals,

Moose

—

A year later, For the Animals had moved its headquarters to Albuquerque, and Cory lived in a duplex apartment with his new girlfriend, Geneva, who worked upstairs in the elephant department. They had a room set aside for out-of-town interns, and summer was their busiest time. During my third internship, I was placed with Cory's cousin Estelle, the in-house film producer. She lived around the corner.

Trudi still wagged her tail when I went to visit, but not like before. I'd been away too long, and it was Geneva she loved now. Whenever Geneva came home, Trudi would run in a circle and greet her with excited yips. Usually, if Geneva was there, Trudi didn't want to go for a walk at all. Some mornings before work, she'd take a few steps with me and refuse to move any further. Then I'd crouch down and strain to carry her, but I could never get far until Geneva passed us on her bike. Once Trudi saw her, she'd follow in Geneva's direction until we reached the office.

Cory often stopped by Estelle's place when he wasn't out of town or working late. One Saturday morning, they were both out on the backyard deck with Trudi and two visitors who'd made the rounds in the office the previous day. I cut up a pineapple in Estelle's kitchen, put it in a bowl with some strawberries for my breakfast, and went out to join them.

"Personally, I don't have a problem with euthanasia," one of the visitors said. "I think it's great."

His name was Benny, and he was the leader of a vegan association in his hometown. I'd missed the first part of the conversation, so I wasn't sure why they were talking about euthanasia.

After a brief pause, Benny added, "But only if you would euthanize a human in the same situation."

Estelle seemed annoyed, defensive. She was a quiet woman, and it wasn't like her to show anger, but she spoke sharply to this outsider.

"There aren't enough homes for all those animals," she said.

But Cory was unfazed. He already had a response prepared, and he welcomed the chance to make his case.

"Well, if you tried to euthanize all the homeless people in New York City, their friends and families would get upset. Plus, they'd *know*—they'd know you were killing them. It's different for a dog or cat. To them, it's like going to sleep."

He went on to tell a story I'd heard before. The accident happened before my time with For the Animals, but not long before. Hundreds of chickens were injured after a truck flipped over on the highway, and the local humane society had shown up with a veterinarian and a few of Cory's colleagues. For the Animals had recruited volunteers to hold the birds for their injections, then put them in crates to die.

"They had a vet who was a total rock star when it came to euthanasia," Cory told the two visitors. "She signed off on a lot of euthanasia orders. But not all of them—the company got some birds back, and the ones they got back were sent to slaughter. I wish I'd known how to euthanize, if only to get it done faster, because those birds were in agony for hours."

"Did you save *any* chickens?" asked the other visitor. Her name was Bora, and she was studying to be a vet.

"The point wasn't to save them," Cory answered. His voice was neutral, matter-of-fact. "The point was to euthanize them so they wouldn't have to go through hell. But Daisy Novak, the woman who runs the Precious Feather sanctuary, was in town for a conference, and she took as many chickens as she could take. And then—"

There was a dramatic pause before Cory finished the thought. "*She left,*" he said. "I couldn't believe it."

After that the conversation fizzled out, with Estelle backing Cory and the guests politely disagreeing. Then Cory called Trudi and attached her leash. As they walked out he glanced over at my breakfast, which I was still eating.

"That's a big bowl of fruit," he said.

—

Thanks a million for sharing your great ideas with For the Animals! We simply couldn't function without the collective wisdom of our wonderful supporters. Your suggestion that we establish one big fund and divide it up among the various animal charities is especially interesting, but may prove to be somewhat impractical in the cold light of day. We're still glad you wrote in to tell us what's on your mind. Don't hesitate to write in again if you have any more ideas for us.

For the Animals,
Moose

—

Little by little, Trudi warmed up to me again. One day I was walking her on my lunch break when we passed a squirrel lying flat in the middle of the road. I looked away, but before I did I thought I saw the squirrel blink. Not knowing what to do, not sure if I'd really seen what I thought I had, I went back to the office and told Geneva.

Geneva walked back with me to the spot where the squirrel was lying—terrified eyes still open, chest moving rapidly, legs spread in all directions.

"Can she be treated?" I asked. "Can she go to a wildlife center or something?"

"I think she should just be euthanized," Geneva said. She sounded sure of it. Still, I walked away hoping for a different decision from the third floor.

"Hey, Moose," she said at the end of the day as I was getting ready to shut down my computer. "I just wanted to thank you for your help with the squirrel."

I looked up. Had they changed their minds and found a rehabber after all?

"We euthanized her," she added when she saw my expression. "She went very peacefully, just closed her eyes."

Bora stared at us from across the room.

"Why?" she asked.

Geneva seemed taken aback, as if Bora had started picking her nose right there in front of everybody. "Why did the squirrel have to be euthanized, you mean?"

Bora walked over to where Geneva was standing, just by my desk. I wanted to shut down my computer because I was finished for the day, but instead I fidgeted with my pile of member correspondence.

"I couldn't help overhearing that an animal was killed here in this office," Bora said. "I'd like to know the reason."

Silence.

"She was paralyzed," Geneva said after a moment. "She got hit by a car."

"Didn't you take her to a hospital?" Bora asked.

"She was too far gone for that," Geneva said. "She never would have been able to walk again."

"But how would you *know* that?" Bora asked. "Unless a vet examined her, and took X-rays, and did other tests?"

She was raising her voice, and other people in the office were staring.

"Humans get into accidents all the time, and sometimes they have to learn to walk again," Bora continued. "Not being able to walk right after an accident doesn't mean anything. It doesn't mean there's no chance."

There was another uncomfortable silence while Geneva collected her thoughts. "That kind of treatment isn't feasible for wild animals," she answered coolly. "I've worked as a rehabber before. Wild animals with serious injuries are put down immediately. They're so afraid of people that it would be cruel to put them through tests, surgery, physiotherapy, who knows what. Plus, most of the animals would be put down anyway because they couldn't survive in the wild. Better to do it now than after months in captivity."

I looked at Bora. So did everyone else in the office.

"That's *bullshit!*" she yelled. She had tears streaming down her face. She ran out into the hallway, and I wanted to go after her, but I didn't.

Bora and Benny began packing their things that weekend to catch an early flight home. Before they left, I went to see them at Cory and Geneva's apartment. I thanked Bora for saying what she had.

"Why didn't *you* say anything?" she asked. "Everybody

just stared at me. Does everyone here think like Cory and Geneva and Estelle?"

"If I had the money, I would have taken the squirrel to a vet," I said weakly. "But maybe a vet would have said the same thing."

Bora stopped packing and began pacing the room. Benny didn't look up from the clothes he was folding.

"I hate this fucking place!" Bora said. "Benny doesn't have an office at home. Benny doesn't get a salary from the veggie group. He works part-time at a fruit stand and lives in a shithole with six other guys. It's disgusting."

"That's terrible," I said, feeling stupid.

"He only eats one meal a day! But a rich group like For the Animals can't even pay a vet to help a sick animal?"

"You're right," I said, but I'm not sure she heard me.

"It's *unbelievable*," said Bora, looking out the window at the quiet street below. "I saved for a year to come here, to learn about speciesism and how to stop it. I paid for my own ticket and Benny's ticket, too. I will never, *ever* support this bullshit group again."

—

Wow, it sounds like you're holding up amazingly well under pressure. Not many of us could handle that kind of stress, and you must be a very strong person. If you feel threatened or think someone might be planning to hurt your beloved cats, I suggest calling the police. I've enclosed our Cat Safety Tips and I hope you'll find them helpful. Stay safe.

For the Animals,
Moose

—

Cory and Geneva must have hosted ten or fifteen interns at their apartment that summer. Most were college students, and one had taken cat tranquilizers for fun. I know this because she bragged about it in the van on the way to a protest in Phoenix.

Another didn't believe in giving money to panhandlers because they'd probably use it to buy meat. She told me this in a Phoenix light rail station, on the way back to our hotel room, as I was reaching into my pocket. I tried to argue, but not for long or with much force.

We were all working toward the same goals, after all. All on the same side. I'd tell myself that over and over again, so often that I got sick of hearing it. Still, at times the four or five years between us felt like decades.

Soon Cory and Geneva were planning another out-of-town protest, and this time they asked me to watch Trudi. Estelle went along to film the event.

With her family gone, Trudi lost some of her stubbornness. We took long walks in the neighborhood and saw bats in the park. Strangers would stop and ask about Trudi and say how cute she was.

She was a good listener, too. I used to complain to her about the cliquey interns staying with Cory and Geneva, how annoying they were, how gossipy and superficial. Somehow I knew she understood.

After work one day, I brought Trudi back to Estelle's house and went out for groceries. When I got back, I went in without locking the door behind me.

As I put my shopping bags on the kitchen floor, I thought I heard something. Startled, I went to the door, where a man was standing outside.

He was around my age, I guess. He claimed he knew Estelle and that he'd mowed her lawn. He said he needed to call his mother and asked to use the phone. I don't know why, but I couldn't say no.

I stayed on the porch with Trudi while he went inside. He said I seemed paranoid when I brought Trudi back into the house and left him standing alone on Estelle's porch. And then he was talking about New Mexico and how beautiful the desert was as he stood there with his pants open and his penis out.

Trudi came over to sniff me after I closed the door and locked it. She knew something was wrong.

—

Two days later Cory and Geneva came home and started organizing their next big protest. There was still a pile of unanswered letters on my desk, to be tackled in between film screenings, lectures, tabling events. The notion of calling the police seemed almost as absurd as the thought of looking for sympathy from Cory or Geneva or Estelle.

Instead I did my work, and I took care of Trudi at the office when Cory was busy. One day an angry hailstorm pummeled the headquarters, and I wondered if the building was strong enough to weather it. Was that a funnel cloud in the distance?

"Oh my God."

As soon as the words were out, I regretted them. Scared brown eyes met my own from under the desk, and I sat on the floor to comfort Trudi.

But the funnel cloud drifted away and never touched the stately three-story office. When I said goodbye at the end of the summer, the sky was calm and Trudi looked bored. She wasn't interested in taking a walk, or in my plans to go back to school and start a new career.

"I'm going to miss you," I said.

Those words got her attention. I knew from her sad eyes that she understood.

—

Hang in there! We at For the Animals know just how hard it can be to stay positive when terrible things keep happening to animals all over the world, every single day, with no end in sight. It sounds like you're doing all you can to push for changes and you should be very proud of all you've achieved. As we like to remind ourselves here in the office, "Success is stumbling from failure to failure with no loss of enthusiasm." Never lose that enthusiasm, and never stop doing what you can, no matter how small.

For the Animals,
Moose

—

When I saw Trudi again two years later, she greeted me with a kiss. Cory and Estelle were too busy to talk for long, and the rest of the staff looked new.

By this time I worked for an animal charity in Canada, and I'd dropped by the office after two days on Greyhound buses. Not knowing the way to the conference I'd scheduled vacation time to attend, I'd shown up in the hope of catching a ride.

I got one. The Precious Feather sanctuary was about four hours from Albuquerque, and Estelle took three of us there in her car—Benny, Bora, and me. Benny was one of the conference speakers, and he still lived in a crowded rooming house and took odd jobs in between animal rights protests. Bora had one more year of vet school to go.

Benny made us all laugh that day, singing along with the corny music on the radio and joking about saving the whales. Was it me who put a damper on the jokes?

I can't remember, but he was very kind when he spoke to me. He asked if I was trying to radicalize the conservative charity I worked for, and I told him I didn't see much hope of it.

"I mean, I write for the magazine, but I don't run the place," I said.

"You don't have to be a boss to change an organization," Benny said. "You can move things forward no matter what your job is. Especially if you write for the magazine. You can push for changes from within."

I thought about that for a while, and as Estelle pulled into Precious Feather's driveway Benny's words were still on my mind.

Estelle started filming as soon as she got out of the car. She didn't waste a minute, first squatting to capture footage of the resident birds preening in the sun before moving into the house to set up her equipment.

Later, when it was Benny's turn to speak, he talked about two rabbits he'd saved from an outdoor market in an alley behind the rooming house.

"Now, are you afraid of me?" he asked at the end of the presentation. "I broke the law. Those rabbits were property. I didn't use violence, but I used force. If you're not afraid of me, why be afraid of direct action?"

Everyone applauded. The conference host, Daisy Novak, ran to the front of the room and hugged him. Benny and

Daisy cried together for a long time before she apologized and told everyone to take a break.

—

Precious Feather was on the outskirts of a small town, about twenty minutes on foot from a massive chicken slaughterhouse. When the lectures were done, we marched past with protest signs and found two hens on the side of the road. They'd fallen off a truck, and one was already dead.

Daisy said the living bird probably wouldn't make it to a vet. "Let's just comfort her, give her some water," she said. Later, she cradled the hen's body as we marched on to city hall. Those hens got names, Winnie and Nat, and they were buried at Precious Feather.

Estelle had to film an event in the next town, so she said her goodbyes after the march. There were other groups heading toward the bus station, and I waited in the parking lot with Bora and Benny as the cars disappeared one by one.

"You guys aren't stranded all the way out here without a car, are you?"

It was the fundraising assistant from For the Animals, the one who'd interned there a year earlier and bragged about taking cat tranquilizers.

"Well, Estelle was going the other way … "

"The car's not that big," she said. "You'll have to squish together in the back."

"We can squish, don't worry. Thanks for taking us."

Once we were on the road, the driver spoke to the woman in the front passenger seat. She must work at For the Animals, too, I supposed. "Poor Cory. He's really going to miss Trudi."

"We'll all miss her," said the second woman. "What a little cutie."

"Miss her?" I asked. "Why?"

"Cory's leaving at the end of this month," the driver said. She said it casually, as if everyone knew but us.

Bora and Benny looked alarmed.

"Where is he going?" Bora asked.

"He's going to be working at the New Zealand office. He got a promotion."

Bora was visibly upset. "Why can't he take Trudi?"

"Twenty hours in a cargo hold? An eight-year-old dog? You know how she is. She'd be terrified. The flight would probably kill her."

"So who will take care of her?" Bora looked around for support, first to me and then to Benny. But we were already in front of the bus station.

"I think they're sorting that out now," the driver said. "Don't miss your bus."

—

"What the fuck."

We were in the bus station. At first I thought Bora was mad because I hadn't thought to help her with her heavy suitcase.

"What the *fuck*," she repeated, and that's when I realized she was talking about Trudi.

"You don't think anything bad is going to happen to Trudi, do you?"

She glared at me, as if she couldn't believe how dense I was.

"Come on," I said. "You know how much Cory loves Trudi. I'm sure he'll leave her with someone he trusts."

"Are you fucking shitting me?" Bora asked. "They've been doing this shit for years and now you think they *won't* do it to Trudi? They're going to kill her. We have to do something."

Do something? I looked around and saw a phone booth.

"I could call Cory and ask who's taking Trudi? Plenty of people love her. His mom, his aunt, his cousin—"

Bora gestured frantically. "We can't let on what we heard. We'll never get another chance."

"Another chance?" I was confused.

Benny said something under his breath to Bora, and they talked in hushed, conspiratorial voices for a few minutes.

"There's a new intern at Trudi's place," said Benny, addressing me this time. "We met him last weekend."

"He was sick," Bora said. "That's why he didn't come to the conference today."

I still didn't get it.

"He'll let us in. We'll come up with a story, and we'll grab her."

Grab Trudi? As in steal her?

"And take her where? They won't let her on the bus."

"Forget the bus," said Bora. "We'll hitchhike."

Benny whispered something to Bora, who responded enthusiastically. I heard the names Trudi, Cory, Geneva, and Estelle. I said nothing because I couldn't hear what they were saying.

—

As the old saying goes, "Consider the source." We're not sure how that rumor got started, but we promise we'd never do anything like that. Of course we'd love to shut down the agricultural fair and send all the animals to a sanctuary, but in the meantime we're urging people to go vegan to help break the cycle of violence. To answer your second question, once every animal is free, For the Animals won't have any reason to exist. We're sure looking forward to that day!

For the Animals,
Moose

—

The dog-nappers were vilified all over the internet. For the Animals offered a million-dollar reward for information leading to Trudi's safe return, though there was no mention of where she would go after that. Animal people, from what I could tell, swallowed the story whole. Bora and Benny were branded crazies, animal abusers, moles for industry. Where would they go? I wondered. How would they hide Trudi?

I boarded my bus reluctantly that day, a part of me wanting to join them and help care for Trudi no matter what. At the same time, I still thought they were wrong. It was impossible to believe Trudi could face the needle just like that poor squirrel and so many others—but Bora and Benny were starting to make me wonder. How many times had Cory and Geneva said they'd rather see animals die than suffer?

Benny and Bora went underground with Trudi, and over the next few months, there was a series of slaughterhouse break-ins around the country. The news brought heated speculation on message boards: People said Benny and Bora were behind it, that they'd rescued hundreds of animals.

I never found out if it was true, but five years later I got an email from an anonymous account with a photo of a white-muzzled Trudi stretched out on a soft bed. Four years after that, there was a second picture. Trudi's face was completely white, and she was sniffing flowers in a garden surrounded by people making the peace sign. All the human faces were blurred, but I'm pretty sure two of them belonged to Bora and Benny.

—

There's a dream I had many years ago, when I was part of the movement for justice for nonhuman animals. I was walking past the meat counter in the supermarket, where steaks and chops were arranged on beds of lettuce behind a glass display. Then I looked closely and saw that they weren't steaks and chops but the severed heads of tiny dachshunds, unblinking eyes fixed straight ahead. I screamed, and kept screaming. I couldn't stop myself, even though everyone in the store was staring.

I often think of Benny's words of encouragement that day on the way to Precious Feather. I wanted to believe him, and for a time I willed myself to believe him. But after a certain point, well, you have to face facts.

Time to admit I didn't have it in me. That I wasn't Benny, and I wasn't Bora either. They were both so selfless, so devoted, giving everything and expecting nothing in return. Doing what needed to be done, no matter the consequences, and always leading from the heart. They must have been born with some rare quality that the rest of us don't have, I tell myself now. I never could have walked that path.

—

Nowadays, of course, everything is different. In 2057, slaughtering animals is illegal throughout most of the world, and the holdout nations are under heavy pressure to follow suit. Would it have happened a day sooner if I'd stuck with activism, if I'd kept on bashing my head against the concrete until the concrete split apart?

Not likely. I was a deadweight back then, one of many well-intentioned bumblers impeding progress for the animals.

For the fur babies, I should say. No one says "animals" anymore, as if humans weren't animals, too.

No, it's a good thing I dropped out. New people had to lead the way. To demand change. To refuse to take no for an answer. The movement needed fresh blood.

—

Before I left the graduation that day, one of Foal's friends sat down next to me and asked a favor. Would I speak at one of their antispeciesist advocacy club meetings sometime? Could I talk about what it was like to be a fur-baby advocate way back—you know?

She didn't say "back in those barbarous times when there used to be slaughterhouses in Canada." She didn't have to.

Well, I was flattered and said yes without thinking. Stupidly, I agreed to attend one of their meetings in October, once the school year gets underway and the club has time to regroup.

Why did I do that? After all, what is there to say?

The more I think about it, the less I want to go. I think I'll call back with some excuse.

No, no. Surely there's no need. I'll forget all about it, and they'll forget, too. I won't say anything, and no one will care.

Liftoff

Ingrid L. Taylor

I remember green, and falling, and leaves like fingers brushing my skin. When they take me, I fall again, into white light cold with hard edges. There is no breeze to sway the leaves here. My arms and head ache from the falling.

Bruno had tried to fight them, baring his teeth and lunging at their hands. They looped a wire around his neck and stung him with the tiny darts that made us fall. I never saw him again, but I can still remember his enraged screams fading as his body slumped and they dragged him, limp and senseless, across the floor.

When they carried Iri away, there was no screaming, no darting. I reached between the bars to brush the soft hair over her knuckles. Her arms curled around a starched lab coat, her eyes wide and sunken, nostrils flared. Swatches of bald skin patchworked her arms, where she had plucked the hair, her fingers skipping like biting insects over her body. She was the last to share my journey. After Iri, they brought the new ones, stinking of misery. Their bodies were whole. They had not yet developed the habits that pass the time—the pressing, the plucking, the small self-mutilations that give a fleeting catharsis. Bent and incoherent, they huddled in corners. Their fear soaked the air. I breathed it in.

I endured.

The white coats didn't understand when I asked them to leave me alone. Their gaze skimmed past the movement of my mouth and hands. They shaped me to their world of chemicals and hard angles, taught me to hold my arm through the bars of the cage while they pierced my skin with blood-sucking darts. If I cooperated, I received a sweet bite of banana, a welcome change from the hard biscuits that tasted like dirt. I would have given anything to bite into a tender mango and suck the sticky juice from it. My fingers ached to dig through forest soil, to snap twigs and feel again the roughness of bark. At night I dreamed of green canopies of oak and mahogany, the shadowy shapes of my family around me, the singing of crickets. Everywhere there was life and movement, but when I woke, the chirps were fans spinning desiccated air. My eyes itched and my throat tingled.

Glinting black boxes crouched on the ceiling with red eyes that tracked every motion. Humming frequencies vibrated in my head until the only way to relieve the pounding ache was to press my forehead, over and over, against cold walls. Rough hands hauled me from my cage, poked the muscles of my arms and legs. After they stabbed me, I felt like I was floating, and I fell again. My mother's gentle touch returned in the haze.

In a clearing overlooked by tall trees, a humid breeze settled on my skin. My family had just finished our midday meal. I dozed in my mother's lap, soothed by my cousins' quiet grunts. The broad leaves shaded us from the sun and dappled the earth with shifting light. Beetles hummed, their wings flickering like rainbows.

Heavy boots crashed into the clearing, snapping branches under their feet. My father shrieked at us, and I clung to my mother's back as she ran. Vines whipped my arms and legs as she climbed a winding ficus into the treetops. She tumbled with a silver dart in her neck, still trying to embrace me as she faltered. We fell, crashing through the branches of the tree we had just ascended. My bones jarred as I rolled out of her arms. I gripped her still body and showed my teeth to the looming shadows.

They tied our arms behind our backs and shoved us into hard boxes. I couldn't see my mother, but I could smell her. We traveled over bumpy roads, the pungent exhaust twisting my stomach, until we reached a settlement with hundreds of men. Attuned to the sweet breezes and soothing greens of the forest, the sharp odors assaulted me, screamed danger. I hunched inside a shrinking vortex of color and sound. My heart slammed against my ribs and my insides churned. They pulled us from the boxes. I exposed my teeth again when they took my mother away, her terrified eyes seeking mine, her neck bent over a sweat-stained shoulder.

In a low, windowless building, bald fingers poked me and jammed a needle into my shoulder, making my body loose and slow. I marveled at the tips of their fingers and how their nails were square and flat like my own. My eyelids drooped. I floated through misty partitions. In the darkness, insects crawled into my ears and nose, their wings beating furiously inside my head. The noise was overwhelming. I moaned at the pressure in my ears and pressed my hands to my temples. There were others near me, struggling and crying out. Fear choked the air. We were united in our panic, and it became a living thing that shivered and slunk among us.

When the pain in my head lessened, I realized it was not

me vibrating but the floors and walls. I pushed my arms and legs out until they met resistance. I could not straighten them, nor could I sit up fully without smashing my head. I curled into a tight ball and wished for each breath to be my last, but my lungs kept pumping and my heart kept beating. The darkness amplified the others' ragged gasps.

We were unloaded onto carts and wheeled out into a sparkling cold world. My nose burned with each inhalation. Shimmering white, like nothing I had seen before, blanketed the ground. Huge mountains split the sky, and gray clouds dipped and swirled around jagged peaks. An undertone of anticipation in the dead, flat air excited me. I wished they would let me touch the strange white substance, but a heavy door slammed behind me, and my cart rattled down a dim hallway.

My jailers were not all cruel. One man, Dmitri, spoke gently and called me "Ivan." His lips curled and his eyes crinkled when he said my name. At first, I was afraid of the shapes his mouth made, but later I realized they were meant to comfort me. He touched me through false fingers worn over his pink, hairless skin. Sometimes he brought me special treats, tiny fruits that dissolved in my mouth.

One day they took me out of my cage, but instead of receiving my usual shots, I was taken to a new part of the building. Dozens of instruments stood in rows, lights blinking and whirring. The air sang with metal and blood. Dmitri patted my back and smiled.

"Be brave, Ivan."

They stood me on a ledge in a round room and fastened straps around my body. When the door closed, I was alone in the smothering black.

With a clank, the room turned, and I gripped the slick wall. The room spun faster and faster, trapping me against the side. An enormous weight crushed me, and I screamed as my skin and bones flattened. When the pressure became unbearable, spots of red and blue exploded behind my eyes. This falling was the worst of them all.

I woke on a white bed. Thin wires pinched the skin of my head and chest. I tried to wrap my hands around my still-spinning head, but restraints locked my arms to railings on the sides of the bed. My body was limp, my bones soft and weak.

An unfamiliar voice murmured above, "He did good. He lasted longer than the others."

Then Dmitri's voice: "Yes, I think he's the one."

When they brought me back, I collapsed onto the floor of my cage, my exhaustion so deep that I soiled the spot where I lay. The smell of urine coated my hair and seeped into my nostrils.

Nika scrabbled in the cage next to mine, pressing her body against the bars to get as close as possible to me. She was one of the new ones, and right away she had gravitated to me for comfort. Small and nervous, her long fingers twitched like the stick bugs I used to play with.

Her delicate face deformed as she pushed her nose between the bars. I liked her eyes, warm and broad, like the leaves of a teak tree. She squeaked as I reached through the bars to groom the soft hairs on her shoulder.

I dreaded the spinning room and was relieved when they devised other tasks for me. With wires taped on various parts of my body, I pushed and pulled levers as they instructed. Then they put me inside a contraption that immobilized me, leaving only my face and hands free, and I repeated the actions. When I followed their directions, I was rewarded with a sip of sugary juice from a straw. Dmitri told me I was doing a good job, and I learned to enjoy his praise, but as the days stretched on, his smile deflated, and deep grooves sank around his mouth and eyes.

One day there was an air of suppressed excitement in the lab. White coats swished as men rushed around talking in rapid voices. Dmitri handed me a piece of ripe banana, a rare luxury. I settled into the weird apparatus, its rigid angles now familiar to me. Some men in jumpsuits I had never seen before loaded me into a moving metal box. Dmitri sat beside me, removed his glove, and rested his smooth fingers on my hand. I laced my fingers through his, like I used to do with my mother. His skin was slick.

The floor rumbled, and low white buildings rolled past, their roofs just visible through the window. When we stopped, they lifted me out of the moving box and put me onto a cart, jostling my restrained body. They pushed the cart through broad double doors, and suddenly I was outside. It was a clear day, and I squinted in the bright sunlight. Warm beams hit my face for the first time in years. I sucked in the cold, brittle air, enjoying the sting in my nostrils. In front of me, a silver object pierced the sky. Its shape reminded me of the dart that had struck my mother, and I remembered her desperate eyes as she was carried away from me. The dart in front of me was massive in comparison, and I ground my teeth at the sight of it.

Dmitri stroked my hand and spoke in a calming tone. Were they sending me home, finally, after I had done everything they asked? They secured my contraption in the cramped room at the top of the dart, leaving me alone while my heart drummed in my ears. I was on my back, grateful for the slice of blue sky open in front of me. Clouds meandered into my field of vision, then wafted away.

A powerful shudder surged through the walls. Lights

flashed on panels around me. The world imploded, and an agonizing weight pressed on my body. The sky fractured, swirling gray and then violet amidst a roaring wind. My throat closed, and my lungs were on fire. My bones and teeth rattled.

Heat flamed through my body. My heart banged against my ribcage, pounding so hard I was sure it was going to rip free of my chest. Tremors shook my limbs, and I felt a sudden wetness as I voided my bowels.

The clouds in front of the window cleared to a vast emptiness pinpricked by light. I had seen this before. In the forest, surrounded by the murky forms of my family, I had looked up at countless shimmering lights in a purple sky. Now these lights spun around me. Their crystalline edges cut the velvety blackness. An immense orb, larger than any monkey fruit, floated in the center of them. The vivid blue called to me.

My body cracked, and the fissures spread within me, expanding out to become thousands of pulsing lives, embracing, fighting, living, and dying underneath the verdant canopies that sheltered and fed them. Mothers nursed babies and foraged for insects in the crevices of trunks. Youth tumbled in play, echoing breathy laughter as watchful elders stood by. I saw a million other me's, trapped in metal and concrete, their despair a sour vein through the fractures. I saw another me, in another life, caressed by my mother's fingers, sleeping under the trees with my cousins.

My heart heaved, and the cracks filled with darkness.

Survival Skills

Diane Lefer

Re: Claim 19-A376852110-06

Believe me, I understand that what with the fires, floods, and mudslides, you people are overworked and stressed trying to process claims—though the Woolsey Fire occurred more than seven months ago so you really should be done with that by now, and I do appreciate that your actuarial tables have yet to figure out how to factor in catastrophic climate change, HOWEVER, I have been waiting a very long time for monies due me and I am in desperate need of my insurance payout without further delay!

When I phoned this morning, someone whose name was entirely unintelligible seemed to be saying you require further detail about the incident. I have already provided information, police records, and receipts but I am now complying by writing out the most detailed account humanly possible to refute any imputation of "recklessness on the part of the policy holder." Though I fear this may be TMI, I trust you will come to understand I behaved in the most reasonable, rational, and responsible way given the extraordinary circumstances. I do hope your company will at last be satisfied so that I may have satisfaction.

The events of June 28, 2019

The day started as usual. My cat, Ozzie, woke me a little after 5:00 a.m. I fed him, showered, dressed, put up my coffee, and carried it upstairs to the balcony with Ozzie padding along behind me. My morning routine, dependent only on weather, is to sit there with my phone (to check email and take a quick look at the news) and put on my dark glasses as the sun comes up. I keep a pair of binoculars handy so I can watch the birds at the feeders in my neighbor's yard across the street. There's usually not much variety—sparrows, mourning doves, hummingbirds, lots of hummingbirds when they're not chased away by the crows. I enjoy watching them. So does Ozzie, though he watches indoors from behind the sliding glass, making little sounds of excitement. Sometimes his teeth chatter, which I think is his hunting instinct being frustrated.

This may seem irrelevant to you, but I want my money. I'm someone who's always played by the rules and paid my bills. I bundled home and auto and my (exorbitant) premiums are up-to-date, and now I am being careful not to leave anything out to make it clear that of all the people on the scene, I was without doubt the most responsible (in the good sense) person present.

The morning in question, June 28, I became aware of movement in my neighbor's tree. This attracted my attention, though I assumed it was a squirrel. What next caught my eye were the flowers, white blossoms and smaller pink and red ones. Strange, because my neighbor's tree does not bloom. It is a tall and sturdy—definitely not floral—tree, and it took me a moment to realize the white blossoms came from a nearby magnolia. It had insinuated its own branches, and pink and red bougainvillea had invaded, climbing the stone wall and twining up and around the trunk. It all looked very beautiful, though none of it belonged. Then I saw her.

First just her eyes, the flick of an ear. Then the pink nose and underneath it the white patches that looked like a bow tie flanked with black. She seemed so calm, at ease, in the crotch of the tree, almost hidden by the flowers and leaves, one leg flung carelessly over the branch, one paw lightly touching the bark farther from the trunk where the bough grew slender.

My first thought was *I hope she's not here to eat the birds*. ("What is it with old people and birds?" says my niece. We all need contact with Nature and okay, I'm older than she is, but that doesn't make me *old*!) I reassured myself a mountain lion is not a house cat and surely would be after larger prey. I know, and maybe she understood, that deer do come this way. (Why else would the neighbor have fenced the saplings?) If not a deer, maybe a squirrel, a possum, a raccoon. A coyote? Now *that* would be interesting—dog versus cat!

Please note, I had no prior knowledge of the animal. I called her *she* to remind myself to be cautious. A female with cubs—kittens?—is more likely to be dangerous. You see, I was from the start very aware of the potential threat.

Then there I was, just like the people I love to criticize, in contact with the digital instead of the thing itself as I looked for answers on the web. *Puma concolor*—the old scientific name was *Felis concolor*. More commonly we say *cougar, puma, mountain lion*, and I will use these names interchangeably in this report. (There are still other names, but as they are not current in Southern California, I won't bother with them.)

I love cats, all or most, though I have to say lions and

mountain lions are not my favorites. Think of a cat, a house cat, bobcat, lynx, leopard, tiger with their lush fur and their faces, their sweet little faces. African lions may be king, but I'm sorry, to me they always look moth-eaten with ratty manes. Mountain lions? Sleeker but still not what I call gorgeous, though through the binoculars, this one did have a smart, intent cat face. In her own way, she was magnificent even if not beautiful, and I was stunned into stillness to see her so close.

In an entirely spontaneous way I whispered, "Where did you come from, sweetheart?"

From what I'd just read, I guessed she might have come from the other side of the freeway and now was wary of crossing back again. Other cougars have been hit and killed by cars: P-52, P-18, and P-23. Or maybe the fire that ravaged her old territory and killed P-64 and P-74 left an imprint of terror. Maybe she was looking for food. Live food, because cougars, like P-47, P-3, and P-4, died from ingesting rat poison in the food chain. (If you've wondered, the *P* stands for *puma* and the numbers are for the ones tagged and studied.) Most deaths do come from cougars fighting each other—the males, of course, so it's possible my *she* is a *he*, but they wouldn't be fighting over territory if we hadn't left them with so little.

Honestly, even if *Puma concolor* is not my favorite cat, we still have to take some responsibility—though in general we humans tend not to and frankly that's why we carry insurance. Be that as it may, I cared about that animal on the tree, on the branch.

If you want to know what kind of tree it was, I can't help you there. If you could look up close through binoculars, as I did, and past the shroud of bougainvillea, you'd see heart-shaped leaves with jagged edges. Deep vertical scoring on the trunk—and if you think that's from the cougar's claws, you're wrong. Apparently, mountain lions don't climb. They leap.

In the calm morning, she was simply breathing. I was watching.

That was the right thing to do, to admire her from a distance, but I admit I wished there were a way we could establish a relationship. Not as friends, not as owner and pet, but simply with me as an ally, one who could impart survival skills:

- cross beneath the freeway through a culvert;

- only eat animals you catch and kill yourself;

- remember it's humans that have taken your territory, not other cougars, so don't let them turn you against each other.

Still, who am I to tell a mountain lion how to live? She was alive. She obviously had all the survival skills she needed.

This gives you some sense of my state of mind when my phone pinged. Up to that point, understand, I was watching her without interfering or disturbing her in any way. An alert from Nextdoor: *Mountain lion spotted at 17243 S. Manderley. Keep your pets and children indoors!* Interesting that pets come first. And shocking that, in spite of this warning, within minutes, the lookie-loos began to arrive, many with small children in tow, including two little girls wearing *I heart P-22* T-shirts.

That's when I went outside. Someone had to protect the children. Mountain lions will rarely attack a full-grown human, but children, little children, are recognizably prey. I tried to talk to the parents. Mountain lions are dangerous. P-22 killed a koala at the zoo. This is not the way to love wildlife which, by the way, is how I feel about the moon. What about this fiftieth anniversary hoo-ha! Why on Earth did we ever go there? Scuffing it up with footprints! Love it from a distance, please! Why couldn't we just leave it alone?

So I was thinking about all the damage we humans do, while all the while the crowd kept growing. Ten, fifteen minutes later there were close to fifty people, maybe more, on the sidewalk and on my lawn taking pictures with their phones and calling others, and those others kept coming. All I wanted was to convince them to leave. They heart cougars. Taking selfies like crazy—themselves in every shot, turning their backs on her. That's why I called 911. All I wanted the police or Animal Control or Fish & Wildlife or whoever's responsible to do was please please come and disperse the mob.

This was a rational action to take even if there were unfortunate and unintended consequences which, I note, may actually have resulted from the Nextdoor alert. It's unfair and highly speculative to say what happened was because of me.

You can't understand how crazy it got: police cars, sirens, news helicopters overhead, news crews with their sound men and their cameras. When the leaves on the tree started to shake, I tried to warn people. "Look, she's getting agitated. Can't you see the way she's twitching her tail? Whatever happens," I said, "don't run!"

That's when I met Harry Knox, who turned out to be a little guy in a Hawaiian shirt. I don't know how familiar you are with social media of very minor appeal—he writes the Hard Knox blog, first just writing about his divorce; the reason everyone in the neighborhood knows him, at least by reputation, is he's been knocking (hard) on random doors and interviewing people about how they've overcome adversity. In this case, he'd merely tapped—not knocked on—my shoulder. "Hey, can I ask you why not?" he said.

"Because if you run," I said, "it's only natural for her to chase you."

Talking to him, I had to shout. The noise was deafening. For an animal used to solitude, it must have been unbearable. The cougar crouched, eyes taking us in, body tensed, ready to pounce. The Fish & Wildlife guy stood there with his tranquilizer gun, the cop drew his weapon, people were pushing, arguing, shouting, *Shoot it! Save it! Take it to the zoo!* As though cages are the answer to everything! I was shouting, too: *Leave her alone! Go home!* and at the very moment when she took a graceful leap out of the tree and onto the street, people scrambled to get out of the way while I cried out, *Don't run!* and my mind lit up in bright LED lights with the words I'd just read: *Leave the mountain lion an escape route.*

Thank God for the app on my phone. The garage door slid up, open, and in she ran. I brought the door down again behind her. We were safe, and so was she. Which mattered. Apparently we're sending the cougars of our region into what scientists (if you believe them) call a *vortex of extinction.* They're doomed, but saving her—one vulnerable individual—was the least and only thing I could do.

"Is your car in there?" shouted Mr. Hard Knox.

Of course. I wouldn't park a new car on the street. I think I have a discount with you based on having a garage.

I didn't expect complications. I had just learned that cougars are more closely related to house cats than they are to lions. And I've lived with Ozzie long enough to know a cat likes an enclosed space. It makes them feel secure. Once inside my garage, I expected the traumatized mountain lion would calm down.

Where I went wrong: Animals are individuals, not just representatives of their species. (I'm sure you work the same way, basing risk on average expectations.) As for P-Something in my garage, we could hear her frenzy even over the helicopter noise. We could hear the scratching sound of her claws on metal, the thumps, the banging and smashing.

"Cougars are homewreckers!" Hard Knox shouted in my ear. "Do you keep the door to the house locked?"

At first I assumed he meant the front door. Then OMG, the door from the garage! My own survival instinct (which extends to those I love) kicked in immediately. I rushed inside to get Ozzie (and also my external hard drive, which I placed inside the go-bag I keep for earthquake preparedness). *Ozzie! Ozzie! Here, kitty kitty kitty.* I shook the canister with his treats. I could hear the cougar's powerful body slamming against the door. *Ozzie, where are you hiding?* I looked under furniture. I ran to the bedroom, and that's where Officer Aguilar caught up with me and grabbed me. (You can read his report.)

Officer Gerard Aguilar threw me over his shoulder and carried me outside. I was still screaming for Ozzie. To my relief, we saw him flee past our feet just as Officer Aguilar set me down on the ground and slammed the front door behind us.

Now, you may not know this, but cougars don't roar and cougars don't purr, but they can scream, and they sound like a person when they do, and that was the sound we heard when, I guess, she shattered the door and got into the house.

Through the picture window, we saw her invade the living room. She froze just for a moment, stunned by the impact, maybe even injured. Then the rampage began. She tore up and overturned furniture, knocked paintings off the walls, scattered books, broke my late mother's teacups and my antique clock, smashed the black clay pottery from Oaxaca, flung about the decorative pillows, swung one in her teeth until the stuffing flew out and about, and unfortunate as all this was for me, part of me, yes, wanted to cheer her on. We destroyed her home and so much more, didn't we?

What did Malcolm say about the chickens coming home to roost?

When she came right up to the window, Officer Aguilar drew his gun, but the frenzy was past. She was calm now. She regarded us coolly. She stuck out her tongue. She licked the window then, from affection or in mockery, I don't know. She closed her eyes, tongue pressed against the glass, and I couldn't help it. I started to laugh.

I laughed the way Ozzie makes me laugh, oh, probably a dozen times a day with his video-worthy goofy charm that somehow coexists naturally with his inherent dignity, and I longed for him. He could be lost, he could be scared, and at that moment, nothing was more important to me than finding my cat.

That's why, for what happened after that, as I've explained before, you'll have to rely on other witnesses and official reports. I understand it took several hours till Fish & Wildlife managed to enter my home, tranquilize, remove the intruder, and release her back where she came from in some canyon where she belongs. The crowd dispersed on its own, chased away by boredom while I spent those hours walking the neighborhood—walking, obviously, because deprived of my car—calling *Ozzie, Ozzie, here, kitty kitty kitty*, searching for my beloved animal companion, in vain.

By the time I returned to what had been and hope will be again my home, only Officer Aguilar remained. He explained my house would have to remain sealed until damage, safety, and habitability could be assessed. Please understand, I'm someone who never expected to be maybe, nearly, even temporarily, homeless, and now I need to get home. What if Ozzie comes back and I'm not there?

Once again, I am submitting copies of all receipts, and have added one I inadvertently omitted on July 1, for $1,537.23, which covers my motel so far while waiting for the cleanup, rewiring, new interior door hanging, and necessary debris removal.

So why did a mountain lion wreak havoc in my home? Considering the threat to an endangered species as well as imminent danger to the people congregated in the area, I did what any reasonable human being would have, or should have, done.

It's easy to blame me and ignore the history and the context, some of which I've alluded to above. I do believe there are worse ways to die than at the hands—jaws—of a cougar, a quick suffocating grip on the neck, probably more humane and merciful than we deserve. But I'll shut up. I'll sit and watch the birds. I can go along to get along. Just give me the money.

Flying Home

JoeAnn Hart

Shelley woke to a high-pitched sound and braced herself for a nurse to come swooping in to see if she was dead. She wondered if that was how she was going to know it was over, with one long, shrill beep. But the door did not open in a flurry of protective polyester, and, at any rate, the sound had stopped. The machines that monitored her bodily functions seemed to be blinking and blurting with no special urgency. With great effort, and not a little pain, she turned her head to the window, smushing her oxygen mask against her temple. "Oh! Hello."

A red-tailed hawk was sitting on an iron rod that extended out from Boulder Community Hospital, right outside Shelley's room on the fourth floor. She'd noticed the rod before, when she first arrived another lifetime ago and had enough breath to stand up to look out the window and get her bearings in the world. A narrow side window was cracked open, and it had felt good to feel honest-to-god Colorado air on her skin. But those few steps nearly did her in, and the day nurse, Jeanette, looking like an astronaut in her baby-blue gear, had to help her back to bed. "Nice try, Shelley," she'd said. "But next time, you ring for me."

"I thought you'd say no," said Shelley.

"I will say no. That's why I say, ring for me. The last thing we need right now is a fall."

It was a moot point. After that, she never had the strength again. It took everything she had to breathe, but she was glad she got that one peek. If she hadn't, she might not know about the rod and then have to wonder what the hawk was sitting on, and it hurt her head to think. The rod was probably left over from some sloppy repair, but this big raptor seemed to think it was custom-built for his own private perch. He was a good-looking bird with his dark-brown plumage and eponymous red tail, without which she'd be hard-pressed to say what kind of hawk he was. As it was, she didn't know her male from her female and had to guess. The bird's intense, furrowed stare was aimed not at her—really, who would want to look at her now?—but at the utility courtyard below, where there was a dumpster, and a dumpster meant rats. Probably plenty of them. Pickings were slim at restaurant dumpsters in town what with the lockdown, so rats across the city were starving, ravaging homes in search of food. Before she got sick, she'd seen them out on the streets in broad daylight, taking risks, exposing themselves to danger in hopes of finding food. The hospital dumpster was a good bet for untouched meals. The medical staff didn't seem to have time to eat, and most Covid patients couldn't ingest anything other than fluids by way of an IV. Shelley first suspected she had the virus when she was making coffee and couldn't smell it. By the end of that day, her temperature was over 100, and that night she was on her hands and knees trying to find a position where she could breathe. Eventually she crawled to her phone and called her son, who called 911.

Rats weren't the only ones interested in the dumpster. Crows, those vacuum cleaners with wings, were ripping their way beak and claw through plastic bags of cafeteria garbage, chattering away like shoppers. "Did you see this? Is there any more of that?" They soared across her view with the foul scrapings of hospital trays trailing from their beaks. It was a wonder they could get airborne, they were so loaded. A baked potato shell, some strands of fettuccine, a gray strip of chicken skin. They certainly didn't want the red-tail staring down at them while they scavenged. He might get tired of waiting for a rat to dart out from the dumpster and choose one of them for lunch instead. It was a bird-eat-bird world.

As she gazed at the hawk, a crow suddenly photobombed her view, trolling its nemesis with a swoop. But the hawk was unperturbed and gave the crow a look that could have plucked him bald. "Stay strong, hawk," Shelley muttered from under her mask. Just as her eyes began to flutter closed, the hawk pushed himself off the rod and shot down into the courtyard. She stretched her neck, but she couldn't see if he scored a rat, and she never saw him rise.

Over the next few days, the red-tail and the crows became her entertainment as she struggled to breathe, giving her something to think about other than cement lungs. The hawk showed up on the rod at least once a day, but she never knew when to expect him. The crows were a constant, noisy presence but were rarely in flight where she could see them. Sparrows, who were thugs in their own right, often flew by in intimidating masses.

Sometimes she felt the place was a little over-birded, but they were visitors, after all, something not allowed otherwise. Her son and his family came once, at a prearranged time, and the nursing staff helped her to a wheelchair so she could wave at them from the window. It was exhausting for everyone. Dave held little Bennie in his arms and pointed at her window, which was certainly too far up for them to see anything other than a shadow. His wife, Betsy, was with them, which was alarming. Shelley knew she must really be sick if her daughter-in-law felt she should come along. They stood between the dumpster and a white refrigerated trailer and waved while the crows looked down on them from the budding cottonwood trees, impatient to return. The birds bobbed their heads and flew from limb to limb, making the branches bounce as if the weight of elephants had been lifted. She looked over the crows and beyond the hospital wing to the foothills and the snowcapped Rockies in the distance. When was the last time she had even noticed the mountains?

When she looked back down at her family, they seemed so small. Her only child, her only grandchild. Small, vulnerable mammals. Sometimes she wondered if humans had any purpose at all. Keith, her ex-husband, had said we were here to protect the Earth, but that made no sense. From what she could tell, the Earth needed to be protected from us. In fact, she didn't see where humans fit anywhere in what he called the great web of life. We devoured everything but seemed to be no one's primary food source anymore, unless you counted the virus. In which case, we were toast.

Jeanette came up behind her. "Shelley, we've got to get you back in bed. Wave goodbye." Shelley raised an arm tethered by a blood pressure cuff, and she saw her son mouth something. She leaned to put her ear to the open sliver of window, but Jeanette pulled her back before she lost her balance. She should have charged her phone so they could talk, but, in truth, she didn't really have the breath, and her voice from under the mask would frighten Bennie. It certainly frightened her, but she was grateful it was just a mask and not a tube down her throat. That's what happened when they moved you from a regular Covid room, like hers, to the dreaded ICU. Endgame.

As Jeanette rolled her back to bed, Shelley knew the moment her son and his family walked away because she heard the crows descend on the dumpster again in noisy celebration. She wished the window could open all the way so she could hear them better. The hospital walls were thick, and her breathing filled her ears, not to mention electronic squawks and the noisy hallway. But no matter how loud it got inside, she could always tell when a custodian went outside with garbage because the crows made such a ruckus. A food delivery! And if she was at all awake she knew when the hawk was on his way because a military detail of crows often mobbed him, trying to keep him away from his perch. Once, she saw them escort the hawk off the hospital property. Crows were persistent little buggers. Another time, she woke just as the hawk rose up from the courtyard with a mighty flapping of wings, a limp rat dangling from his claws. As much as she'd been rooting for the hawk against the crows, she felt for the rat. She hoped the end was quick. Suffering was a terrible thing.

She remembered once, when she was down with the flu, Keith trying to get her to sit outside in bone-chilling February weather to boost her immune system, insisting that natural settings were healing and would create a path to her soul if only she were open to the experience. It was such a Boulder thing to say. He was as annoying as a crow sometimes, constantly soul-questing, always trying to improve himself, forcing her to come along. After they got divorced she never hiked again. What a brat she was. What she wouldn't do to be able to hike right now, to have that sort of breath. Funny she should think of him now. Those years began spooling out in front of her like colorful ribbons, the scenes vivid and magical like a movie, and she tried to grasp her younger, hopeful self to keep her from disappearing again. Somehow in the process, she pulled a tube from her arm, and Jeanette came in and loosely tied her hands to the bed with soft bandages, and that was surely for the best.

Later, she opened her eyes, and there was a crow on the rod, looking in at her, first with one eye, then turning to look at her with the other. Or was it a gargoyle? The creature was all beak and wing, hunched over and ugly, spouting words instead of rainwater. "Life is a near-death experience," the bird cackled before flying away.

Oh, no. She was hallucinating now. That couldn't be good. What was that nursery rhyme about counting crows? One is for sorrow? There was some sort of commotion going on in the hallway. She side-eyed the hall window, and there were gurneys everywhere, a traffic jam of the sick and dying. She was grateful to have a bed. She heard a man call out that he was a lawyer. "This situation is actionable," he croaked. "When this is over, there'll be hell to pay."

If only she had the oxygen to laugh.

When there were no birds to focus on, she stared off at the familiar peaks and sloughs of the mountains. Spring was coming. The snow was melting, exposing the scarred landscape along the slopes, still black with soot from the wildfires that fall. That had been a scary time. You couldn't breathe from the smoke and ash. There were other scary times. She remembered going up a trail together as a family and coming across a fresh kill. The bloody contents of a deer had been hollowed out and devoured, the insides ribbed like the roof of a cathedral. *Eviscerated* was the word. She was uneasy knowing there was some animal, drooling red, waiting for them to leave to finish the job. Keith hardly gave the deer a glance, except to remark on the different types of flies on the carcass, and kept on his steady pace to the top of the ridge, but she and Dave stopped to gape. He was only five. "What happened?" he asked.

"Life happened," she said. "It's sad, but the bear or mountain lion who killed the deer needed to live, too."

Dave's eyes grew large. "Is it dead?"

It took a moment for Shelley to respond. What constituted dead if not this? And yet. The blood was wet, and the flies pulsed with vitality, making it seem as if life was just moving from one form to another. "The deer is definitely dead," she'd said at last. "Look at it. It's all eaten away." He squatted to peer into the carcass, and a cloud of flies rose up. "Let's go," she said and grabbed his hand. They continued up the mountain, meeting up with Keith, and then, after she begged, they took a different path back down. She told Keith it was for Dave's sake, but she knew it was for her own.

She'd do anything to hit that trail again, to be in the mountains where life could be reconsidered. To review all the options again. She'd felt like she'd been circling the drain for days, but at least someone had removed the bandages. Maybe the worst was over. Or maybe they had to untie her to flip her over onto her stomach to take the pressure off her lungs. That had seemed to help, but there was no more looking out the window, and the mask dug into her cheeks. A physical therapist came in to help her, as he called it, "visualize her breathing."

"Think of your shoulder blades as your wings," he'd said, putting his gloved hand on her bare back. "Now, pull your breath into your wings and feel them open. Expand your wings, Shelley. Good. Now let the breath go. Fold your wings and relax. Expand, and fold. Again. Good. Open your wings wide, Shelley. Excellent. You'll be flying in no time."

It was so Boulder. But it helped.

In between people coming and going to mess with her, she tried to sleep, but the noise seemed to ramp up every time she closed her eyes. The beeps, the alarms, the announcements. Code this, code that. The crying out. The oxygen machine was so loud. Both she and the machine were working hard. She wished they'd turn it up. She heard people out in the hall say Covid this, Covid that. Wait. Or were they saying *corvid*? Corvid? She pressed her mind into action until it came up with the answer. A crow was a corvid! Counting corvids. Counting crows. Counting Covids. If a group of crows was called a murder, what was a group of Covids called? A slaughter. She laughed, but it used too much precious oxygen, and she started gagging, and Jeanette ran in with a syringe.

> One is for sorrow,
>
> Two is for mirth,
>
> Three for a wedding,
>
> And four for a death.

Later, after a team came to flip her right side up again, a nurse's aide brought her an iPad. "Someone wants to say hello." It was Dave and Bennie, and she sensed they weren't calling to say hello. Dave said he loved her too many times. They were falsely cheerful, so she was falsely fine, then drifted off to sleep in the middle of a sentence. Wild visions, the sound of crows infiltrating everything. Humans in her dreams began to speak in caws and clacks. Telling corvid jokes. A corvid and a rabbi walk into a bar. Then Covid followed, and they never walked out. No one laughed. This place has no fucking sense of humor.

At sunset, the crows were going wild, and she opened her eyes. Something was up. She pressed the button to raise the bed upright. The nurse's aide had left the sides down after her sponge bath that afternoon, so she dragged one leg over the side, then the other. She sat on the edge to let the dizziness subside, then carefully plotted her path so she wouldn't yank out any wires or tubing, not wanting to set off any alarms. Jeanette would not be happy. She took her mask off and tested the air. There was no air, and she put it back on. The clear tube was long enough to get to the chair by the window. Grabbing the metal tree that held bags of fluids, she slowly, excruciatingly, shuffled the three feet to the chair and flopped down on it, gasping.

The crows were gathered in the cottonwoods, their attention on the double utility doors, and rats were leaping out of the dumpster. Garbage must be coming. Dinner. Someone in a black bomber jacket came out and set all the crows to cawing at once, but he wasn't carrying a bag. He didn't even go to the dumpster but walked over to the white refrigerated trailer instead and unlocked it. When he turned to open the door she could read the back of his jacket. BOULDER CORONER. He waved to someone inside the hospital, and two women wheeled a gurney out. They wore the same bomber jacket, like a sports team. The Boulder Coroners. Their slogan: *Nature always bats last.* On the gurney was a white plastic bag, and the crows went berserk. The three coroners quickly maneuvered the body into the trailer, and when they stepped out, one of the women looked up at the hospital and seemed to sigh.

What had Shelley thought was in there? Had she never wondered? The women wheeled the empty gurney back into the hospital while the man stood guard at the trailer, and they rolled out another body bag, and then another. The crows settled. Finally the man closed the trailer door and locked it, and the team went back into the hospital, and the double doors closed behind them. One by one, the birds raised their wings and floated down to the dumpster.

Alpenglow radiated pink behind the mountains, and she yearned to be walking the foothills, to be awash in that healing light, to be so high up she could turn around and view her life at a distance. She wondered if she could locate that trail again after all this time. She wanted to find the spot where the deer had been and collect the weathered bones in a pile, then top it with the skull. She wanted to sit and wait for the mountain lion who'd killed her, who surely watched her every move and knew exactly where she was. There was a lightness in Shelley's chest, and she felt herself glowing with love for them both. She wanted to grab them together and hug them, like they were family.

She really needed to lie down. She had to get back to the bed, but she wasn't sure how. She'd used up all her strength, and the call button was out of reach. She should just stay where she was and wait, but she had to lie down, now. She could do this, she thought. She'd done it before.

Shelley did not know how she ended up on the ground. She did not remember falling. Jeanette ran in and said, "What the hell," and called for help on the intercom. Shelley's mask must have slipped off because she couldn't seem to breathe. More nurses in protective gear arrived and surrounded her. One nurse pushed the chair out of the way and glanced out the window. "I hear they have to bring in another trailer."

"Don't be looking out there," said Jeanette. "Get me the paddles."

Shelley didn't know what the rush was. She wasn't in any pain, although she sensed her body wasn't arranged quite right. Maybe her wings were in the way. She heard a long shrilling sound.

"Oh, the hawk," she thought. "The hawk is here."

One Trick Pony

J. Bowers

DATE: 31st AUG, 1938
SCENE: 2B
TAKE: 12

Jesse James's getaway horse won't jump off a cliff, no matter how fast ace stuntman Cliff Lyons gallops her, snorting, toward the yawning edge.

For four hours now, the film crew has been working on this stunt, destined to be the equestrian centerpiece of *Jesse James* (1939). They've tried whips and spurs, hollering and waving, even threw lit firecrackers at the little mare's hind legs, hoping to panic her over. Now they have her wearing movie blinkers: serene equine eyes painted on a dainty headstall, invisible in an extreme long shot. Tricks just like these have taught us horses in the Wild West loved to china-shop through saloons, collapse over trip wires, and soar boldly off fifty-foot cliffs under heavy gunfire—so utter was their devotion to the American cowboy.

But ace stuntman Cliff Lyons is careless on his first approach—he doesn't gallop fast enough, giving his mount time to notice the land is ending. All twelve subsequent jump attempts have ended with the little mare skidding to a halt, crow-hopping, and shaking her mane at the abyss: a hard no.

On the shore below, Twentieth Century-Fox Film Corp. contract director Henry King's threadbare patience frays. He's spent six months preparing to shoot five seconds. By rental helicopter he scouted the ideal ratio of sublime crag to rangy poplar, consulted depth charts. Anachronistically poured in 1931, decades after the James Gang rode the range, the manmade Lake of the Ozarks remains the only deep-water lake in Missouri. It rests several counties away from the production's home base in sleepy Pineville, Missouri, where a starstruck city council let his crew bury Main Street in fill dirt and nail wooden facades over the storefronts downtown: Justice of the Peace, Acme Tool Company, First National Bank of Northfield. Due to these and other on-location expenses, Henry King's budget for *Jesse James* (1939) is already over a million dollars, and climbing each second this goddamn horse doesn't jump off that goddamn cliff.

Seven cameras idle along the lakeshore like skeletal waterfowl, necks craned toward the lapping water, lenses black and waiting. Not for the first time, Henry King wishes he'd hired one of those diving girls he and his wife saw in Atlantic City to double Jesse instead. Some skullcapped waif in a red bathing suit would have already sailed that goddamn horse right off that goddamn cliff, easy as a paper airplane. Dress her like Jesse, tape down her gymnast chest, and no audience would spot the switcheroo—they'd be watching the horse, collective breath well and truly taken.

The epic shot Henry King imagines is somewhat out of

character for a director barely footnoted today in accounts of classical Hollywood. To some degree, his lackluster reputation can be blamed on the saccharine dramadies Twentieth Century-Fox gives him: soapy pap like *I Loved You Wednesday* (1933) and *Seventh Heaven* (1937). Less director than recorder of deeds, Henry King's "aesthetic" is a vague barrage of shot-reverse-shot, malingering close-ups, and medium long interiors. He frames shots like he's filming a play—a common error of directors who came up during the silent era, nimbly avoided by the likes of Alfred Hitchcock and John Ford, King's more famous contemporaries. Even he can tell these men are destined to win at history, making him an also-ran. This is why he spends most nights drunk and alone on his terrace, the lit white letters of HOLLYWOODLAND gleaming like starlets' teeth from the black hills beyond.

A proud Virginian by birth, Henry King was intrigued by screenwriter Nunnally Johnson's barstool pitch to recast Southerner Jesse James as a hero, not an outlaw. He liked the idea of the notorious James brothers as just a couple of good, God-fearing guys driven to crime by the transcontinental railroad's unjust seizure of homesteaders' land—just the kind of heroes post-Depression America wanted. "About the only connection it had with fact," said Jo Frances James, Jesse's elderly granddaughter, "was there was a man named James, and he did ride a horse."

Twentieth Century-Fox heartthrob-in-the-making Tyrone Power would play Jesse. Brunette ingenue Nancy Kelly signed on as Jesse's estranged wife Zerelda, while up-and-comer Henry Fonda took the role of Frank James. Veteran character actor Ernest Whitman, whose filmography includes roles such as Colored Gentleman (uncredited) in *Buck Benny Rides Again* (1940), King Malaba in *Drums of the Congo* (1942), and Black

Man Talking To Himself (uncredited) in *The Lost Weekend* (1945), portrayed Pinkie, the James boys' loyal Uncle Tom. Though Whitman gives a fine performance, the character is a clumsy attempt to whitewash the family's Confederate past. Whitman reprised Pinkie alongside Henry Fonda in *The Return of Frank James* (1940), making him one of the first Black actors in Hollywood with a franchised speaking role, but this accomplishment is not what *Jesse James* (1939) gets remembered for, when it is remembered at all.

Studio head Darryl F. Zanuck greenlit the picture despite concern making Jesse James into a Depression-era Robin Hood would doom it everywhere but Missouri, where the infamous train robber already enjoyed folkloric status. Undeterred, Henry King insisted he shoot on location in "real James Gang territory," an expensive 1,563 miles from Hollywood, claiming the verdant Ozark backcountry would set his new movie apart from the five other Westerns being filmed simultaneously in the usual desolate corners of Nevada, New Mexico, and California.

Zanuck agreed. "It's hard to ruin a Western," he said, signing the papers.

Now, on set, those words ring in Henry King's ears like a double dare. He slaps another mosquito dead, grinding its wiry body into the black hairs sprouting from a large mole on his right arm. He thinks about how Henry Fonda and Tyrone Power are being paid to nap in Airstream Clippers instead of playing Frank and Jesse James in Twentieth Century-Fox's new Western—the first ever shot in three-color Technicolor. He squints at the lowering sun. By now he should be shooting Frank James scrambling onto the opposite shore under heavy but inaccurate gunfire. Or Jesse James treading water under a green tangle of ivy, left for dead by Frank, galloping off-screen as bullets rain the lake. Cut to Henry Fonda and Tyrone Power toweling off for the drive back to Pineville, the shot safely in the can.

"Goddamn horse is burning daylight!" King barks at no one in particular.

Among the poplars, assistant key grips scatter like startled quail.

DATE: 31st AUG, 1938
SCENE: 2B
TAKE: 14

The goddamn horse now in question is named Babe, though this is known to no one on the crew of *Jesse James* (1939) save ace stuntman Cliff Lyons, who trained her himself as part of the stunt string he boards on Twentieth Century-Fox's backlot, where Babe spends half her life.

The rest of the time she's surrounded by humans who wear too-clean clothes and shout at each other, her nose stuffed in a feedbag and her tail in a manure catcher until she's requested on set. Though uncredited, Babe has been background scenery in Roy Rogers's *Under Western Stars* (1938), marched in several studio parades, and performed a feature stunt in the Republic Pictures serial *Zorro Rides Again* (1937), where she leapt a five-foot-wide gully without complaint, Cliff Lyons himself in the irons.

But today he's asking too much. As apex prey, every horse's brain is wired to protect the herd from hazards exactly like the cliff the humans keep trying to force Babe over. The fear of the first horse they tried hangs in her nostrils. When the herd says *don't go*, you don't—she learned this as a foal. Babe tries to convey this law with bucks and snorts and kicks, but this is a semaphore ace stuntman Cliff Lyons can't or won't understand. When Henry King barks "action," Cliff claps his legs against Babe's sides, and together they charge pell-mell down the trail leading to the jump-off. The little mare likes this part okay: The footing is soft for a gallop, and the trees streak by in an agreeable green blur. Down the stretch they come, horse's knees pumping, man's torso rigid, braced for flight. Then Babe skids to a halt thirty feet shy of the edge just like she said she would, flinging ace stuntman Cliff Lyons into a twisted, cussing heap.

When he sees the stunt still isn't happening, Henry King stalks uphill, swinging his megaphone like a billy club. He is the unfortunate sort of person who cries when he's mad, and his eyes are swimming by the time he reaches a bloody Cliff Lyons. The cowboy dabs a scrape on his brow with his red bandana and explains how there's no sense in trying again today. Maybe not even tomorrow—the horses are too rattled. It'll take six hours round trip to get another one from his stunt string. There's a buckskin gelding in Pineville yet who might do. But not till tomorrow: He won't haul horses in the dark.

Henry King takes a deep draught of piney Ozark air and squeezes his eyes shut, sending tears down his sweaty cheeks. He believes in a version of himself who can calmly explain how he needs to see two horses leap like Pegasus, black hooves treading cloudless blue. He wants to (gently!) remind Cliff Lyons the trick he's failed at fourteen times is supposed to be the equestrian spectacle of this movie, the sequence to make cap gun–toting schoolboys *ooh* and *aah* and pester their friends to go see the new Jesse James picture again, two horses dive right off a cliff, it's swell!

Instead Henry King aims his megaphone at Cliff's square jaw and screams he is the worst goddamn stuntman in Hollywood, a sham and a cheat who needs to get back on that goddamn horse and do what he's being paid for, right goddamn now. Blinking, Cliff Lyons spits in the dirt, staring King down like he's just another ornery horse needing a come-to-Jesus moment.

Unlike Fox contract director Henry King, ace stuntman Cliff Lyons's career and reputation hangs on the movie he made last week, not last year. He is sunburnt and sore, with a hot shower and a cold beer waiting for him back in Pineville. This may help explain how and why Cliff Lyons, whom history otherwise records as a thoughtful and humane horseman, ever agreed to what happened next.

DATE: 1st SEPT, 1938
SCENE: 2B
TAKE: 15

Invented by industrial agriculture to slide unwitting livestock into cloudy troughs of flea dip, the tilt chute is a steel platform enclosed on three sides by pipe railing, with a gate on one end to let animals in one at a time (cattle) or en masse (pigs, sheep, goats). The three-tiered railing prevents stock from escaping until the operator pulls a lever and the platform tilts, spilling the animal(s) into the drink. Once dunked, the bathers scrabble to their feet, shrugging off the chemicals, then trot up a corrugated ramp, making way for the next victims. Used correctly, the tilt chute is quick and humane.

It is also what Henry King and/or Cliff Lyons—blame is hazy—used to slide poor Babe into a dead drop seventy feet high. Greased with lard, a tilt chute is the reason why, in the final cut of *Jesse James* (1939), Frank and Jesse's twin horses are not seen triumphantly soaring into open air, a trumpet fanfare heralding their graceful descent. Instead we see them falling, one horse after the other, in the same awful posture, silent and wrong.

The lead-up to the stunt looks spectacular: A posse thirty lawmen strong pursues Jesse and Frank at full gallop, soundtracked only by stampeding hooves and birds chirping. The James boys are faster; they develop a slight lead. Pulling up both horses, Frank James dismounts to make sure his brother's up for what's coming next. Jesse's been shot in the arm; he's in shock.

Henry Fonda reaches up to shake a woozy Tyrone Power awake in the saddle, slurring at him to keep going, keep going—his leading man looks twisted in agony as Fonda urges him to hang on tight, that there's only one way out of this.

Tyrone Power feebly nods, clinging to his saddle horn like a child. Quick cut to the lawmen gaining on them, their horses thundering around the bend the James boys just rode through as gunshots pepper the trees.

"Gee-yap!" hollers Henry Fonda, pretending to whip Tyrone Power's horse with a branch. As Power gallops off-screen, cut to ace stuntman Cliff Lyons galloping downhill on Babe until a strategically placed log forces her to jump.

Cut to a wide shot of the cliff: A quarried hulk of lined limestone dominates the right half of the movie screen. The way the camera is angled transforms the Lake of the Ozarks into a canyon river, obscuring the water beyond. Bushes on the blufftop rustle, and the stunt starts there, with Babe coaxed into a rear to make this look like a running jump. Then the tilt chute slides the mare's hooves out from under her, and she drops. Crouched in the bushes beside the chute, ace stuntman Cliff Lyons jumps right after, windmilling black-jacketed arms to steer himself away from the horse as she backflips through empty blue space, forelegs tucked into fetal position, limp as a failed kite.

Cliff Lyons knew the plan ahead of time, so he is able to somersault into something resembling a dive before he hits water. Babe isn't so lucky. Her head jackknives backward as she smashes the surface; the splashdown is enhanced in post-production by a foley artist punching a bucket somewhere in California.

Before the audience can react, cut to Cliff and Babe leaping over the log again, then a closer shot of the same stunt from a slightly different angle. This time Cliff's supposed to be Frank, not Jesse, and Babe is supposed to be Frank's horse. The fall is shown in grisly instant replay. Again we see the horse's spine chop the sky like a guillotine blade, visual déjà vu.

Cut to a bird's-eye view of two wet horses paddling alongside a gasping Cliff Lyons as Frank James. Henry Fonda clambers ashore with them under heavy gunfire, then mounts one of the horses to gallop off-screen, leaving his brother for dead.

Meanwhile, Tyrone Power surfaces under a canopy of branches, concealed from the posse descending to the riverbank, his survival unsurprising.

Everyone knows Jesse James doesn't drown.

DATE: 1st SEPT, 1938
SCENE: 2B
TAKE: 16

Marketed by Twentieth Century-Fox using taglines like "Motion Pictures' Supreme Epic!" "The Tremendous Dramatic Thrills of the Midwest's Lawless Era!" and "So

Big and Sensational! Yet Capable of Stirring Your Tenderest Emotions!" Henry King's pet Western premiered in New York City on January 14, 1939.

Early reviews were generous. *Variety* commended the movie's "consummate showmanship … pictorial magnificence … skillful and seasoned direction" and the "superlative performances" of its young cast, particularly Power and Fonda. The *New York Times* declared the film "the best screen entertainment of the year" and "an authentic American panorama, enriched by dialogue, characterization, and incidents imported directly from the Missouri hills."

Not one critic praised or damned or even mentioned the film's cliff dive set piece, which is odd because the stunt is all *Jesse James* (1939) gets remembered for today, when it's remembered at all.

Of course, Henry King's cameras were still running when Babe resurfaced. Instinctively, she tried to right herself, legs thrashing at bad angles while ace stuntman Cliff Lyons swam ashore. Still in character, he didn't look back until he knew he was off-camera, since Frank James would have cared more about not being shot than what his horse was up to. When he did get a chance to look, Cliff Lyons was surprised to see his horse dead, bobbing like a buoy in the middle of the lake. Some eyewitnesses swear they saw her back snap on impact, the water a brick wall. Others insist she died of panic: Too disoriented to know she should be swimming, she tried to run.

Either way, ace stuntman Cliff Lyons rowed out with the life-jacketed production assistants to dispose of the body the same way he'd dealt with drowned livestock during his ranch-hand days. Babe's mane sculled like seaweed in the murky lake water. Cliff Lyons undid her soggy saddle and bridle, dragging them into the rowboat's bottom. Then he held the mare's stiff pasterns together so the PAs could tie on the rock he chose, a thick slab of gneiss left over from when the lake was dug. It was quiet on the set as the little mare sank, her grave first marked by a bubble column, then nothing at all.

A horse dying on set is the sort of accident a better director would have written out of their movie. A different man would have found another way to get the James boys off the cliff and into the next scene. But because he was stuck in the silent era, Henry King felt audiences wouldn't understand how both Frank and Jesse made it over the cliff without seeing the stunt happen twice. As he saw it, the only alternative to reusing the fatal footage was an unfinished movie.

In the cutting room, the director reviewed the cliff stunt enough times to develop a blind spot three seconds long. As a result, Henry King was honestly shocked to learn that at the glorious zenith of his epic Technicolor Western, in matinees across America, grown adults and children alike covered their faces or choked on sodas, wide-eyed.

When confronted by the American Humane Association about the stunt, Twentieth Century-Fox studio head Darryl F. Zanuck maintained that although they did "lose" an animal during production, no horses died on screen in *Jesse James* (1939), which is true. Henry King's camera averts its guilty eye just after splashdown, like a father turning our heads away from something awful, fooling no one.

The Pet Project

Helia S. Rethmann

The first people Molly and Kate expose to their Get Paid to Have Her Spayed pitch are wealthy clients Molly considers friends. They meet at an expensive restaurant that is decidedly old-world. Patrick and Daniel—white, privileged, male—blend effortlessly into the surroundings; Molly and Kate do not.

Molly is wearing a pilling sweatshirt from her college rowing days, the logo of her team long washed out, and rubber clogs practical for walking on frequently disinfected surfaces. Kate doesn't notice the shoes (or the shirt) until the hostess shows them to their table and she sees Daniel notice them. Immediately, Kate's cheerful Guatemalan sweater becomes gaudy and cheap. Her front teeth are too large. Molly's eyebrows are overgrown, and when did Molly stop plucking her whiskers?

Daniel's strained silences during dinner are easier to take than Patrick's fake laugh. Kate drinks her wine too quickly and tells herself that she and Molly are too busy for vanity. They are here to make a pitch, collect, and get out. For their good cause, Molly and Kate can deal with many things, including having a side salad for dinner (the only vegetarian option, hold the bacon bits) while watching the men suck on pieces of live-boiled crustaceans. The end justifies the means. But the end, when it comes, is not at all what Molly had promised.

"I thought Patrick was an old friend?" Kate says, tipping the valet who brings their car around five precious dollars. The valet barely nods.

"We go way back," confirms Molly.

"They can throw away fifteen hundred dollars on a blood panel to rule out genetic diseases for Rufus, but they can't afford a basic pledge? Some friends." Kate puts the car into drive and pulls away from the curb. Another car honks, and Kate slams on the brakes. Molly falls forward.

"Careful." Molly rights herself. "Do you want me to drive?"

"I'm fine. Do we even charge them for office visits?"

"We do not," Molly says.

"They said your idea was brilliant. If it's so brilliant, why won't they contribute?" Kate's back mirror shows a blur of lights. She has trouble seeing the lanes in front of her. She's either going night-blind or she had too much wine. Probably both.

"They're still paying off their wedding. It was an elaborate affair. They said they'd help out when they could. Patrick's law office isn't going so great. Hard times for everyone." Molly is rooting through her messenger bag.

"What are you looking for?" Kate watches her wife and accidentally runs a red light.

"Eyes up front! Pay attention. I knew I had something to eat in here." Molly brandishes a power bar. Unwraps it.

"Patrick's law office is doing just fine. Divorce is always in season," Kate says. "Can I have some of that?"

Molly extends the chocolate-covered log, and Kate bites down on it. Chews. Has a hard time swallowing. They have two more days to raise the money.

"They chose that place. They should at least have picked up the check," Kate says.

"They should have," agrees Molly.

—

Asking rich friends for money is annoying enough; asking poor friends is intolerable. That's why Kate never sent the donation link to friends like Becca and Eric. She is surprised when she checks the GoFundMe page on Sunday morning and finds Becca has contributed $100 with a note—*Not much, but everything helps?*—and three emojis with heart-shaped eyes. Eric has given money, too.

"We have to pay them back," Molly says when Kate tells her. "Isn't Eric on food stamps?"

Kate nods. "And Becca's unemployment ran out. We can't give it back without humiliating them. The question is: How did they find out?"

Molly peels off the gloves she wears to rub sulphurated lime into the mangy coat of their newest dog tenant and gives Butters a treat. The kitchen smells like the bowels of hell. "A friend must have forwarded it to them. It's a small world."

As of 10:40 a.m. Sunday, the donations on the fundraising site total a bit more than half of what's due in rent for the new facility come Tuesday, but nothing approaching their insane budget, which includes paying for two helpers and the assistant vet Molly hired, plus medical supplies. Kate gets up and raises the kitchen window as high as it will go. She inhales the cool March air.

"We'll use our savings until we can get more publicity," Molly says. "Every start-up struggles."

What Kate wants to mention but doesn't is that they only have enough in savings to pay their mortgage for three more months. What Kate would like to suggest but doesn't is that she and Molly continue to work at the clinic part-time. Alec would take Molly back as his partner. It's not going to happen. Molly—when she burns bridges—burns them all the way. Come Tuesday, they will be on their own: swim or sink. On the bright side, Butters's coat is growing back.

—

What neither Molly nor Kate foresaw (why didn't they?) was that if you pay people for getting their pets spayed or neutered when they drop them off, said people may not return to pick up their pets at the scheduled time.

By 5:00 p.m. on their first day, Molly and Kate are left with four drowsy cats and two dogs. They wait a while longer. Kate admits that her enthusiastically designed Owner's Contact Information sheet has flaws. If Turner Avenue 34 in Madison, Tennessee, is not a valid address and 615-888-1234 is not a valid phone number, Brian Schmuck might not be an actual person.

"That was just plain stupid of us," Molly says. "We need to hold off on the money until pick-up time. Can we change the wording on the website? And on the waiver, so there won't be legal issues? Let's ask everyone to show some ID."

LaToya, one of the helpers, takes home a kitten. No one else offers.

—

Kate and Molly don't have enough rooms in their house to keep the temporary lodgers in solitary confinement. They're not about to force animals having just undergone surgery to socialize with other recovering animals, let alone the rowdy full-time residents.

They put the three cats in the guest bathroom in their cardboard carriers and let them out one at a time to be petted and fed and to sniff their neighbors at leisure. This way, the cats can get comfortable with each other and become best friends by morning. Some hissing and mournful meowing is to be expected.

The two dogs—a giant poodle mix and a terrier with a clipped tail (Molly has named him Poor Thing although the name on his intake form was Chris)—are sleeping it off in the bedroom. The full-time residents are not thrilled by this development. They are used to sharing Molly and Kate's bed and their smells. They can't get settled on the living room couches. Their barking is frequently interrupted by grievous howling, and Butters, confined to the mudroom, chimes in.

"I'm going to kill somebody," Kate vows, returning from letting the dogs out into the garden and in again for the fourth time.

"On the bright side," Molly says, "there is such a demand! We used less anesthesia than I thought we would. Dr. Stanton is a pro at this! And most people pick up their animals."

"It's gracious of them," Kate says.

"We're on the front end of a national emergency, if not a global one."

One of the full-time residents is scratching the bedroom door, whimpering.

"You don't have to sell me on your fundraising pitch," Kate says. "I'm already sold, remember?"

Molly turns the sound machine to the loudest ambient noise setting and snuggles closer. "Just remember, love," she breathes into Kate's ear. "Every day we're doing this, we're making a dent in reducing the homeless population to come. A small dent, but dents add up. Soon enough, nonprofits will spring up all over and follow our business model. You'll see."

Kate hopes so. Ever since people began traveling and going out again, abandoned pets are everywhere. Packs of skin-and-bone dogs roam the grocery parking lots. On country roads, the number of slain cats outnumbers all other roadkill. It's sickening. And yet. And still. They are only Molly and Kate, four arms and two hearts between them. Who are they to change the trajectory of the future?

—

A good number of people don't carry an ID when they drop off their pets to be fixed. And what is Kate supposed to do? Send them home to fetch their papers, as if they were cheating first graders instead of adult people down on their luck? The facility is in a poor neighborhood, a veritable United Nations of the disenfranchised. The last thing people being denied their voting rights need is a white woman challenging their identity. So, every time LaToya asks if the pet of a person without valid ID should be accepted, Kate says, yes, yes, yes; admit him/her. Some of those cats and dogs, Kate fears, will not be picked up at 4:00 p.m. There's little comfort in being right. At 5:00 p.m., five more cats and three more dogs appear to have been permanently abandoned. What now?

Dr. Stanton, the other vet, cannot possibly take home another critter or her husband will kill her (why marry such a jerk?). Chrissy lives in a building where pets aren't allowed. LaToya takes home another cat but is not happy about it.

—

Every shelter or rescue worth calling is filled past capacity and not accepting incoming animals. Kate knows this. The shelters and rescues were the first to alert Molly to the crisis. Kate tries them anyway; they have friends in these places. Her calls go straight to voice mail. "We are sorry to let you know that you will no longer be able to leave a message at the end of this recording," a wobbly voice at the end of the Second Chances number is saying. "Too many of you are telling us you'll have to put Fido down if we can't take him in, that we are your last option. Your calls are upsetting the staff because we can't help you. There comes a point when a rescue can no longer adequately care for those entrusted to it because it's stretched too thin. Second Chances reached this point a while ago. If you wish to adopt an animal, text 555-541-2021 and await instructions. To make a donation, please use the link on our website. Thank you for caring."

"What a mess," Molly says when Kate plays the recording for her. "And a reminder how vital our work is. I wish we could hire a third doctor to pick up the pace."

"Meanwhile, what are we to do about these guys?" Kate motions to the cardboard boxes.

"We can't very well leave them alone overnight," Molly says. "They need to be monitored."

—

At home, their teenage pet sitter howls when she sees Molly and Kate carry in more boxes.

"You're kidding, right? More asshole people didn't pick up their pets?"

"That's right, Jayden," Molly says. "Give us a hand with the crates?"

Jayden answers with the exaggerated whole-body sigh reserved for the pure moral outrage of the young.

"I fuckin' hate people," she says once the cats in their crates are secured in the guest bath and the dogs in their carriers in the bedroom, which involves a lot of door-holding and door guarding and the shooing away of excited residents.

"Me and you, and Molly, too," Kate says.

"Leave me out of it." Molly makes Jayden sit on a couch in their living room. "Tell us how your day went."

Jayden takes in a gulp of air and looks from Molly to Kate, and from Kate to Molly. She never releases the breath. Instead, she starts to cry. "It went horribly. It was a horrible day. Nobody was happy."

Spiked hair and skull tattoos notwithstanding, the insides of Jayden are mush. Molly hands her a tissue, and Jayden rips the tissue into the tiniest of tiny pieces, which Kate will have to pry off the braided rug on cleaning Saturday. For now, Kate mutes her objections.

"What happened?" Molly asks again.

"The cats aren't getting along at all." Jayden sobs. "I took the three new ones to the catio, like you said to. I opened the crates because it seemed like they wanted to go out, and two of them came out and everyone started fighting right away. They were running up the walls and Mayor's claw got stuck in the screen door and when I tried to help him down he scratched me." Jayden holds out her forearm, displaying three raised red lines. "It burned like hell."

"I bet," Molly says. "Did you put peroxide on it?"

Whatever they may have told the girl, sleep deprived as they were this morning, letting the cats out had not been on the agenda. Jayden intercepts Kate and Molly's worried look and responds with defiance: "I took off their stupid cone hats. The cats hate them! Kate told me males don't really need them that long. You guys tell people to keep them on only to be extra careful."

It's true. Kate had said this at some point.

"The Elizabethan collars can prevent serious complications," Molly starts, but Kate shakes her head *no*.

"The black-and-brown-and-orange-and-white one is still wearing hers," Jayden says. "She never came out of her cage."

"The calico," Kate clarifies. "She hasn't let us touch her either. She's very shy."

"Yes," Jayden said. "She never left her crate."

"She's still in it?"

"Far as I know." Jayden wipes her nose on the arm of her sweatshirt.

As for the dogs, they were fine, but bad in a different way. Jayden walked them both in turn, and the poodle pooped as soon as she let him inside. The sausage dog threw up on their bedspread, which Jayden has put in the wash.

"Sounds like you are due for a pay raise." Molly yawns and offers to drive their pet sitter home.

When they are gone, Kate defrosts a mystery microwave meal and pours herself a large glass of wine. While whatever-it-is cooks, she feeds the residents and checks in on the bathroom cats and the catio. Mayor is perched on the highest plank, growling at invisible intruders. No sign of the calico, who must still be in her crate. Kate turns off the lights. Back in the kitchen, the permanent residents keep getting under her feet, but Kate has no energy to pet them. Butters is yapping forlornly from the mudroom, due for another walk. *There comes a point where we can no longer adequately care for those entrusted to us,* Kate thinks, *because we're stretched too thin.*

—

Good news! Channel Four, the favored local channel, is interested in running a profile of Get Paid to Have Her Spayed—if approved, their segment will air on the six o'clock news.

"We're going prime time, baby!" Molly dances Kate around the recovery room. "Nothing like free publicity! A major network picks up the story and—boom!"

Kate's eyes roam over the cheerless industrial space. "Should we maybe hang some pictures?"

—

Jayden has decided to stay in the office/storage/guest room for now. Whatever schoolwork she has, she can do on the old desktop, and she doesn't mind the ratty couch. She can help out a lot more without the commute. Kate and Molly don't argue. "As long as it's fine with your parents," Molly says. Jayden assures them her folks are glad to be rid of her.

The pet sitter brings the calico into the room with her. The cat still hasn't left her crate, but earlier Jayden got her to eat and drink some. She prepares a little bed with towels from the linen closet and puts a litter box next to it. She scents both the bed and the litter box with generous helpings of catnip. "You can come out now, Callie," Jayden croons. "You're safe in here."

"You've named her Callie?" Kate asks.

Jayden blushes. "For now," she says.

—

Kate wants Molly to go over talking points with her. She's nervous about the news team; they have to get their story right.

"They are the ones who have to get the story right," says Molly, administering the smelly salve to Butters. She talks to the dog in the high-pitched cartoon voice that bubbles up when she's in good spirits. *Look at how handsome you are, you handsome prince. Aren't you just devastatingly handsome? Yes, you are*, etc. "Jayden offered to post profiles of all the adoptable animals on the website. I saw the one she made about Callie. Heartbreaking picture of a terrified cat in a crate: *I'm scared and why wouldn't I be? I need someone to restore my faith in the world.* It's a good idea, don't you think?"

Kate agrees.

"I wonder what happened to that little girl to make her so terrified," Molly says.

Kate is confused. "Jayden or the cat?"

Molly thinks. "Both," she says. "Either."

—

The news team, when it shows up early the next morning, is comprised of a small, brisk woman by the name of Amanda and two burly guys handling the camera and lights.

"Just go about your business like you always do," Amanda says. "We'll shoot some footage to be edited later, and then we'll interview you. Just act normal."

Acting normal when the large red eye of a professional camera is trained on you is harder than Kate expected. It doesn't help that Amanda seems impatient; the journalist snaps at the lighting guy for taking too long to set up and at the camera guy for framing the wrong shots.

"Get her giving her spiel to the people!" she screeches. By *her* she means Kate, who is explaining the intake forms and procedures to the day's group of pet owners. Kate's eyes blur, her voice quivers, and she hears only mumbles in response to her questions. Her body is out of control. Handing off the patients to LaToya and Chrissy with the red eye and Amanda watching becomes a high-wire act, her hands are shaking so much. It's 8:30 in the morning, and she is ready for a drink.

Molly walks and talks as she always does. "If you're going to zoom in on the shaved parts, have the decency to block out the faces," Kate hears her joke from the operating theater. A male voice laughs. The crew interviews Molly as soon as the surgeries are done and before they leave on an extended lunch break.

"How did it go?" Kate sticks her head into the operating theater, where Molly and Dr. Stanton are monitoring vital signs. Molly shrugs. "Hard to say," she says. Dr. Stanton rolls her eyes.

The patients are asleep in the recovery room when the crew comes back. It's hours yet until pick-up time. Amanda instructs the sound guy to affix a clip-on microphone to Kate's sweater.

"Say something," she tells Kate.

"Hello?" Kate says.

"The sound levels are crap," Amanda tells the sound guy, who immediately re-affixes the microphone, touching Kate in all the wrong places.

"Hello," Kate says again.

"Better?" the sound guy asks.

"No," says the journalist. "Let's get it over with."

Kate is queasy with … fear? Exhaustion? Self-loathing? She no longer knows how to construct a sentence.

Amanda instructs the cameraman to hover over the cardboard boxes and counts out loud: "Thirty-one, thirty-two, thirty-three. Tell us, Kate. How many of these boxes do you think will be left tonight?"

"Eh … what?" Kate says.

"How many of these animals will not be picked up by their owners, or rather people who pretend to be owners for the twenty-dollar cash reward?"

"Hard … to … say?" Kate fixes on Amanda's eyes to steady herself. Amanda's eyes go from irritable to tetchy. "Can we stop bullshitting for a moment? Molly told us the two of you are currently fostering twenty-one animals left here. When you already have five cats and seven dogs at home. It sounds a lot like *hoarding*, is what I'm saying. What makes you think that Metro's impulse to euthanize is wrong? How can this possibly turn out all right?"

Kate's mouth opens, but no words come out. When they do, they come out in an incomprehensible gush.

—

They watch a replay of the six o'clock news that night, once the newcomers have been taken care of. Local politics, a drive-by shooting, a lengthy profile of the new police chief. Their segment never airs.

"They must have changed their mind," Molly says.

"I fuckin' hate the media," says Jayden.

Kate feels relieved. They share a microwave pizza and two bottles of wine. Jayden's three years away from twenty-one, but if the girl is mature enough to deal with the cruelty of existence, she's mature enough to have a smallish glass of cabernet to take the edge off her day—another challenging one.

Two hours later and three glasses in, Kate feels like herself again. She is in her *zone*, a place where few things matter. The television is on real time now, and between a commercial for a laxative and another one advertising erectile dysfunction relief, the slick host of the upcoming ten o'clock news chimes in with a teaser: "You won't want to miss tonight's Channel Four exclusive! The news is next."

Jayden, the only one watching, squeals, "'Molly against Metro'! That's you, guys!"

Molly has fallen asleep with two of the longtime residents on her lap. Jayden shakes her awake. "Our story is on!" Jayden shouts into her ear.

Kate focuses her eyes on the large screen to see someone who looks like her hand out hardback boards to a group of sleepy people. "Anyone else need a pencil?" the person resembling Kate cries. "If you don't know your pet's date of birth, guesstimate it." The person resembling Kate then repeats the same two sentences in botched Spanish.

Real-life Kate closes her eyes and pretends she's dreaming. But she can still hear the voice over narration: "Every day from 7:15 a.m. to 8:00 a.m., between thirty and fifty cats and dogs get dropped off at a facility north of the city with an attention-grabbing name: Get Paid to Have Her Spayed," the voice of Amanda is saying. "In the hours that follow, these animals will have their reproductive organs rendered unproductive. They will be lovingly cared for by Doctors Thompson and Stanton and staff before getting picked up by their owners or people who pretend to be their owners for the sake of the twenty-dollar cash benefit. The cash payment has been reduced twice already, down from the initial fifty dollars a patient. And still the pets keep coming."

Kate opens one eye. There's footage of a ragtag line forming in front of the clinic. People hold animals in their arms, in blankets, in carriers. LaToya comes out and yells at everyone to leave their critters in the car until the paperwork is done. Kate's opens her other eye.

"The idea is, of course, to reduce the homeless pet population, which has grown to an alarming size since the end of the pandemic." An emaciated pack of dogs is seen ripping through garbage bags behind a pizza franchise.

"The idea is to prevent the city from euthanizing thousands of animals who lack care and shelter." An Animal Control worker places a half-frozen cat in the back of her van.

"Cats and dogs bearing the mark of having been neutered or spayed are usually spared and given the benefit of the doubt." A close-up of the little green tattoo Molly and Dr. Stanton use to mark the recently fixed is followed by footage of Molly talking to a sleeping dog of undefinable heritage. "There now, little buddy"—Molly's cartoon voice is heard—"you're all set, my sweet prince. I swear you won't notice the difference, or not right away, anyway."

Kate lets out the breath she's been holding. "This isn't so bad, or is it?" she asks the other two people in the room. Jayden shakes her head. Molly stretches and readjusts the dogs on her lap. "I don't talk like that to you guys, do I?" she asks the dogs in singsong.

"It's a bold idea." Amanda is shown for the first time, sitting behind an official-looking desk. She's newly glamorous with lipstick, powder, and mascara. "It's just outrageous enough to work. But will it? Can it?"

Amanda gives the eye of the camera a long stare. Behind her, on the screen, is a still of the day's recovering patients in their enclosures. "In spite of the cash payment, many of these animals will never be picked up. Some that are picked up are immediately released again by their so-called owners. By the end of each day, a good number of them will, simply, be left." Now a shot of a pitiful kitten behind bars fills the screen. Not one of their patients, Kate thinks, nor one of their cages; the image was likely hijacked from the archives of the Humane Association. Amanda gives the camera a little sigh, shaking her head.

"Way to milk it, woman," Molly murmurs.

"You may wonder what happens to the pets who don't get claimed," Amanda continues. "Will they be surrendered to Animal Control? Adopted by Good Samaritans? The answer will surprise you. You'll find out just as soon as we come back." The screen goes to commercial break.

Molly puts the dogs on the floor, one after the other. "I'm tired," she says, getting up. "Is there a way to record this? I need to turn in."

"You can't!" Kate and Jayden scream in unison. Molly sighs and sits back down. The same two advertisements keep playing on a loop for what feels like hours.

"I'd rather die from the conditions than the side effects," Kate observes.

By the time Amanda comes back on, Molly's nodded off again.

Amanda, behind her desk, starts by summarizing the story for those who are only tuning in right now. Then she's on to the all-important question: "Where are the abandoned pets now, you want to know? As of this reporting, every animal left behind during the first week of the project is being fostered by Dr. Thompson and her wife and partner, Kate. If you picture a hobby farm with lots of acreage, think again. Dr. Thompson and Kate live in a small home on the outskirts of town, with a very modest front yard. When they leave the house every morning to do their life-changing work, they leave behind an ever-growing number of dogs and cats. A young helper named Jayden is in charge of the critters until they return—with more animals."

Kate groans.

"Hey!" Jayden shouts. "They said my name on the news!"

The camera footage is zooming in on their front yard now: Too many dogs are sniffing and rooting around, pooping, and getting into fights. Here's a shot of empty water dishes. The space looks crowded and out of control, a dog version of the Coliseum after Hurricane Katrina.

"Nobody authorized that woman to shoot out here!" Molly is sitting up, acutely awake. "It's an invasion of privacy! Did you tell them it was okay to film here, Jayden?"

"I swear, I never saw them," the girl says.

"It was me." Kate is suddenly sober. "I may have told them our address. I was … I don't remember exactly what happened. She was so mean … so bossy. I—"

"Christ's sake!" Molly picks up an afghan that has slid off the chair and shakes it before throwing it on the couch. A thick cloud of dust and hair rises. "I'm going to bed."

—

For most of the night, Kate lies awake, awash in misery and waiting for sounds of Jayden retching in the bathroom. Kate should not have allowed the girl a second (third?) glass of cabernet after Molly went to bed. She's a terrible role model— no role model at all. But Jayden never retches. Instead, it is Kate suspended over the toilet come dawn, puking her guts out until no guts are left. Molly tells her to stay home; Chrissy will handle the intake.

When Kate, spent and shaky, enters the kitchen, Jayden has made toast and scrambled eggs.

"Just coffee," Kate says. "Was Molly in a bad mood when she left?" Kate accepts the mug Jayden hands her.

"Not that I could tell." The girl is gleaming. "Guess what? Callie slept with me last night! I woke to find her on my chest, and then I fell asleep again. When I woke up, Callie was back in the box. But it's a start, isn't it?"

"Mm-hmm," Kate says. Jayden was probably dreaming. "Did you reconnect the phone?"

As soon as their segment had aired last night, the landline started ringing. Kate and Jayden had thought it best to unplug it.

"Not yet. Should I?" Jayden is throwing pieces of egg to the dogs in the room.

"No." Kate sips her bitter coffee. Her cell phone, charging on the kitchen counter on mute, vibrates with important information. Kate enters her passcode. *You have forty-three unread messages,* the phone informs her. Kate wants to throw the thing in the trash.

"I'll help you out today," she tells Jayden. "What do we do first?"

"We need to change the litter boxes in the catio." Jayden piles too much egg onto her toast, and some tumbles to the floor, where the residents fight over it. "The toilets are really smelly." Jayden chews contentedly. "I think we're out of fresh litter?"

—

What a relief to stroll down the aisles of the clean, well-lit superstore and not be followed by animals. What a treat to accept tiny samples of food not covered in dander! Kate tries the miniature spinach pastry and thimbles of tomato soup. Her stomach feels much improved. She and Jayden fill the cart with essentials and a few luxury items, and Kate hopes her Visa card won't be rejected. Both she and Molly had to take out cash advances in recent days. But the friendly woman at the register swipes the card without a hitch.

"You're legal, all right." She smiles as she hands back both the Visa and Kate's ID, required for purchasing five boxes of wine. But then her expression changes. "Wait a minute," she says. "I know you! Where do I know you from?"

Kate freezes while the woman makes the connection between her face and the merchandise. "You're the lady who was on TV last night! From the dog hoarding operation!"

Her eyes roam over the fifty-pound bags of dry dog and cat kibble, the stacked cases of wet food, the multi-packs of cat treats and chicken jerky. "Looks like you're feeding them well."

"We treat them well, too." Jayden is loading their purchases onto a trolley.

"Oh, I don't doubt that, pet!" The woman snatches back the chicken jerky and runs it through the scanner again. "There, now. I marked the bags damaged. Takes fifty percent off. Not much, but everything helps, right?" She winks at Kate.

—

Kate prepares vegetable lasagna for dinner, Molly's favorite, but before that, she and Jayden clean the house. They vacuum and dust. They change the litter on the catio and go on whole-yard poop control.

"Just like an Easter-egg hunt, only less festive," Kate tells Jayden as they scout for turds under the bushes, and Jayden laughs.

They play with the cats and walk the dogs. They disinfect all surfaces and wash all bedding. Neither the frantic activity nor Jayden's affability can calm Kate's nerves. She'll have to talk to Molly tonight about her breakdown, her on-camera freak-out. *I've become a liability,* she will say. *It appears I'm not suited to stress at this level. The last thing I want is to hurt the operation. Sully your reputation. Stand in the way of salvation.* She tries out different phrases, finds them all equally ridiculous. *I didn't mean what I said to that woman,* she will say. *I wasn't myself.*

Who were you, then?

Kate is chopping vegetables to be roasted: onions, carrots, zucchini, peppers, squash. The red sauce is boiling. The dogs are outside, where it's raining again. Jayden is preparing the dogs' dinner; quite a few of them are on special diets, but Jayden has no trouble keeping up. The dogs bark when Molly's car drives up. Kate sticks the roasting pan in the oven and turns the sauce to simmer.

"We better give her a hand with the cages," she says to Jayden, wiping her hands on her pants. But Molly, when she comes to the doorway, is not carrying any boxes.

"What happened?" Kate is looking past Molly to Molly's car, which Molly locks with a *beep* of her key.

"Volunteers!" Molly gives Jayden a hug and kisses Kate on the cheek. "You would know if you bothered to answer the phone."

Kate and Jayden exchange a look; they'd never reconnected the landline.

Molly stomps ahead of them to the kitchen, surrounded by wet and excited dogs. "Smells good!" she says, petting the muddy-pawed animals. "There were about twenty people when we closed shop. All eager to foster. They wanted to pay to foster. Not enough animals for everyone. I told the disappointed ones they could swing by here tomorrow and have a look around."

"Volunteers?" Kate watches Molly's rubber shoes leave impressive track marks on the newly clean kitchen floor.

"Yes! Volunteers! And more pledges." Molly lifts the lid of the saucepan and inhales. "Are you making your famous vegetable lasagna?"

"Who pledged?"

"Who didn't? Patrick and Daniel pledged double for the year. They also want to take in two dogs and a barn cat. They have the acreage, and we already know they're responsible. I knew they'd come through."

"Oh," Kate says. She's feeling light-headed.

"That's great! I'll go check the website." Jayden disappears into her office.

Molly inspects the bowls of dog food on the counter and shrugs. "I don't know who gets what," she says. "I guess they can wait a bit to eat."

Kate pours them both a glass of wine. Molly sips while Kate gulps.

"Everything happened because you said that shit about euthanasia being the more humane option," Molly tells Kate. "I was upset when you said it, but it did the trick. Brilliant marketing strategy."

Kate wants to correct the record, but where to begin? "I didn't mean it," she says.

"'Course you didn't." Molly clinks her glass against Kate's. "Point is, it worked. To us!"

"To us," Kate repeats.

Jayden reappears from her bedroom. "Bummer," she says. "Only four people clicked on the profiles, and none of them offered to adopt. But guess what?" She fishes a tumbler from the dish rack and holds it out to Kate.

"What?" Molly prompts while Kate fills the girl's glass.

"Callie came out soon as I sat down. Purred on my lap for a bit. I think she likes me now."

"'Course she does," Molly says, scratching the back of Poor Thing. "Now, listen. Here's a thought: With things picking up, we need to hire a third vet ASAP. And scout for a second location. Any ideas?"

Kate's eyes roam her recently clean kitchen and settle on Poor Thing. The tailless terrier is investigating mud prints and chooses the moment to poop on the floor.

Behind the Chokecherry

Jacquie Vervain

SWINE & CHEER FESTIVAL: DAY 8

When your body is chopped up and ingested by seven
strangers, and your blood is left to dry in the dirt and shit
beneath a desert juniper in the midst of a now-empty field
through which flies are swarming lazy and swollen in the heat,
it becomes a challenge to focus complete attention on any one
place and time for very long. But to put a spin on what Mother
said during that sweet week before she was taken away and
we were put in the pen, what doesn't entirely obliterate your
consciousness from the face of the Earth makes you stronger.

And so I prefer to look at this new state of mine as an
opportunity for spiritual growth and worldly experience,
rather than as a tragedy of the utmost mundanity. We always
knew it would come down to this, Ava, and after seven years
in the swine yard pen, minus one eventful week in a hanging
cage tied up in the town square downtown with the rest of my
doomed herd, it's quite a nice change of pace to be out and
about, free from all my personal pain and suffering, lurking,

in part, deep inside the tingling body of Sariah Flint, second wife to the holy and hallowed Prophet, the venerable Gideon Flint, as she washes the breakfast dishes at her sterling silver kitchen sink, the water blistering her raw, red hands as the morning's sun comes in thick through the window.

Sariah ate my feet up yesterday, one enormous and sloppy bite after another, then moved on to my snout. Normally it's all proper and prim with Sariah, having been raised in the temple by a mother whose dearest desire for her only beautiful daughter was to marry quick and marry high, but when Sariah gets anxious it settles her tender nerves to stuff something in her mouth. Anything, really—my body, cold and drained of blood and hooked up to the ceiling of the butcher's crowded shop with a spike three inches thick, just happened to be the closest edible object when Sariah saw Eliza Flint, the holy and hallowed Prophet's first wife, walking through the festival's crowds toward Sariah's location at the picnic table where their fourth-youngest daughter was blowing bubbles with a purple wand. I can't really blame Sariah for eating me. Eliza is a terrifying specimen. Even secondhand, the slant of her eyes gives my soul a slight chill, though I'm not quite certain what about Eliza's appearance caused Sariah's anxiety to peak on this particular occasion. Her memories are all around me here inside her skin, but they're swirled up like stardust in the sky, like bubbles in a pool recently jumped into. All I know for certain is the nerve running up the length of Sariah's left arm tightened taut when she saw Eliza, as it's tight right now at the kitchen sink. The whole limb is uncomfortably numb as her neck and spine tingle in between the hollow vertebrae she can feel every time she raises her hand above her hip. The memories inside my own spherical soul are less disjointed than hers outside the circle of me, and your face is clear as the moon on a cloudless night, Ava, but the space between the blowtorch in the field they ran me down into and Sariah's stomach is a black thick void.

———

Bridger Rigby ate my jowls and shoulders late yesterday afternoon, after soccer practice ended and he and the other boys biked over to the festival to throw firecrackers at the girls' feet as they braided one another's hair into increasingly stupid styles. Opinion on the morality of Hagoth's Cross's annual Swine & Cheer Festival is divided. Mr. Rigby loves the way the pork tastes fresh off the silver hook with wild adrenaline coursing through the dead cells of the sizzling meat. Nothing compares to the electric sensation of that first juicy bite, and after a whole year of adhering to Mrs. Rigby's standard low-sodium, low-cholesterol, low-sugar menu, plus all the days he rejects offers from his business partners to go out and get a drink, smoke a cigar, play some cards, unwind, he feels it's his right to go out and eat a whole pig if he pleases. Bridger Rigby firmly agrees with his father, and though his mother clucks her tongue and shakes her head at the savagery, Bridger has spent the better part of the past seven days downtown at the festival, eating pulled pork and bacon and sirloin and sisig and ribs and hock and tenderloin and trotters and belly and chops and sneaking Pepsi and watching the races and the eating contests and the pig-squealing championships.

Today, though, Ronan Young came to soccer practice and told Bridger and the rest of the soccer boys that he heard about a truckload of dead chickens floating down the river. Bridger's just now realized he's sick of the planned festivities. When he was in elementary school last year, he and all the other boys thought it was radical to watch a man yank the teeth out of a howling pig with a set of rusty pliers before impaling her left eye like a grape tomato with a samurai sword they later saw at a garage sale on Brigham Lane, but now the whole thing is starting to feel stale and boring like everything else in this town, this world. Bridger craves something he doesn't quite understand. I think it's probably chaos he wants, chaos he's chasing down on his bike, his thin thighs burning as he pedals up the slanting asphalt road to the river.

I don't think it's chaos he's chasing. I think he just wants to see those dumb bastards float down the river like the clucking fools they are. I sure do.

Bridger? I ask in confusion, thinking perhaps the boy has detected my presence inside him, thinking maybe I won't have to be alone inside him.

It's me, Craig!

Ah. The boy ate you, too?

Cooked me up like bacon for breakfast.

—

I'd forgotten how it felt to be inside another, contained and warm and safe, until I awoke from the void and found a part of my pink soul floating in Sariah's belly, along with the bubbling remains of a sour Pepsi, which she most certainly should not have been drinking, which she is now regretting as she wipes sweat off her brow and fiddles with the air-conditioning control panel. I'd hoped I'd find you on the other side, Ava, but alas: Here I am, and here you are not.

Looking back now, the three months inside Mother's belly when I was just a little burgeoning piglet were the most comfortable of my life, and so it wasn't really all that bad to emerge from death into this quasi-familiar space. Those months inside Mother's womb weren't the happiest, though—those came later, as you no doubt know, when you were brought to the swine yard from that charming farm where you'd grown up. You started off that first day just like all the days to follow, telling me stories you'd learned from the books little Sookie Zabriskie read to you, back before she fell into a well and her family sold the farm and all the livestock off to pay the lawyer to prove that Mr. and Mrs. Zabriskie did not conspire to push their daughter into the well.

But I'd rather think of all the various methods of torture celebrated at the Swine & Cheer Festival, many of which yours truly and eternally and unyieldingly, Amos Throckmorten III, was subjected to, than those months we shared, Ava: tooth extraction, mutilation, flagellation, castration. Also: flaying, kneecapping, branding, stoning, boiling, impaling, hamstringing, strangling, bone-breaking, raping, scalping, sawing, foot-roasting, denailing, hanging, and don't for a second underestimate the power and the pain of a plain old-fashioned and unimaginative beating.

—

Dallin Gubler, the farmer who owned me before I gained my belated freedom, slurped my ground-up bones down in a spicy soup he ordered for breakfast this morning before the sun came up hot, after having eaten my belly and my head yesterday afternoon. He's entering Cornelius in the Big Pig Contest in a few hours, but he's worried that Cornelius isn't quite as large as Stockton Taylor's entry. When Dallin's peewee football team lost the championship, his father didn't let him eat for a week. Dallin's tied Cornelius down with rope that cuts his soft, spotted skin and stuffed a plastic tube down his throat, like how he used to methodically shove an eraser down the length of a plastic mechanical pencil during classes at the temple, and now he's pouring sand through a funnel into Cornelius's hulking belly so that he'll outweigh all the others and Dallin can take home the red sash and hang it on his wall with the one he earned last year, and the year before, and the year before that one, too.

—

Sheriff Spencer Kimball came in third in the Sausage Eating Contest last night, swallowing down every single link of my organs and blood and guts packed in a casing made of my intestines. There are so many voices inside Spencer I can't quite make any single one of them out.

—

Sariah's done with the dishes and is now scrubbing the floor with a sponge and a bucket of soapy water. Suds move under her fingernails, loosen the skin. The air conditioner is out, and sweat is running down her tingling spine. Eliza always scrubs the ever-gleaming floors, but today they're filthy, caked with ground-up Cheerios, squished bits of asparagus, and crumbled pretzels. Sariah's thinking about first wives, how they always want everything their way, and they usually get it without even seeming to have wanted things their way. It's a trick that combines a little logic with a saccharine-sweet tone into a series of simple sentences that have all the other wives thinking the first wife only wants what's best for everyone.

And she does. What's best for everyone is what's best for Eliza, and so it's hardly a trick she has to play—it's more of a tilting of reality that sends everything rushing through gravity's magic straight toward her wide, gaping mouth.

—

Bridger pedals up the hill, adrenaline coursing through his young body as he thinks about the dead chickens floating in the river. The last time he saw Uncle Wyatt was at the river. Uncle Wyatt kept telling Father he could hear God like a foghorn in his skull. Father said stop, this isn't going to end well for you, think of the kids, your wives, the store. Uncle Wyatt said, I'll prove it to you right now. All three of them went to the river in the warm slow twilight, and Uncle Wyatt proved God was talking to him, but still the Prophet called him apostate and made him leave, and now he's on that stupid show, and all the boys give Bridger a hard time about it, so Bridger's planning to grab one of those dead chickens right out of the water and throw her at Ronan Young's fat face as soon as he gets there. A preemptive measure. The eggs Bridger ate for breakfast are chirping low and so distant I can hardly hear them at all.

—

The field where they ran me down with pitchforks and daggers through the chokecherry is the only place I can go to be alone and think just my thoughts. My blood is all over the dirt, mixed in with my shit. When it dries and disappears, I don't think I'll be able to come here anymore. You told me the soul takes seven days to realize its own death and move on to the next world. You told me everything I ever knew about anything outside the shitty pen. I don't want to go anywhere without you, Ava. I don't want to always have to think about the pen when I think about you. I remember the day you came in like it's happening now. Maybe everything is always happening now.

They keep the herd in a room that smells of darkness, pressed up close to one another so there's no space to move or stretch or take a deep breath. Not that any of us wants to breathe deep. Craig's to my right, his padded shoulder pressing into my throat, my always full, hard belly smashed up against his thigh. Randal, my mortal enemy for offenses far worse than any of this, is in front of us with his wide ass pressed up against both our faces. I crane my neck up at a strange angle that's hard to keep without generating a sharp black migraine, but better the ache than that the shit fall from the center of Randal's prodigious rump and spill straight into my mouth like yesterday, and the day before, and the day before that, too. Usually shit falls into my mouth at least a few times a week. It's been a bad week, but little do I know how fair and just and balanced the universe always is. Fluorescent lights shine down from the ceiling, ring my ears. Freddy's to my left, his leg trembling against mine. Last week Vincent's legs gave out and he fell and we all had no choice but to step atop his convulsing body and get on with eating our slop.

Later they came and took him. They'll eat his flesh, I'm sure, but it won't taste as good as ours will at the festival. Dallin Gubler always says it's important to follow protocol, if you want the results to yield success. My ass is pressed up against Sean's ear, but most of the time I forget about Sean entirely since I can't see him, though sometimes my tail twitches against his ear and I remember we used to curl up next to one another beside Mother and dream the same witless piglet dreams.

And then there's a shift and a roll and a reshuffling to the room and you are beside me, Ava, your skull pressed up against my temple like we're a pair of Siamese twins. I look up at the desert juniper and wish we'd been born a pair of Siamese twins and we could have spent the whole world together and I wouldn't be alone in this shit bloody field wondering where you are, whether we'll ever wind up together again.

—

The voices of the other barnyard animals inside Sheriff Spencer Kimball fade a dull gray as the small snippets of the various souls settle and drift elsewhere. Spencer hasn't been able to do anything at all today except lie in bed while Taylee rubs his back and brings him ginger ale. Taylee's his fourth wife. He wanted to stop at three, but when Wyatt Shumway started running his mouth about how God was talking to him even though everyone knows God only talks to one man at a time, the one true Prophet Gideon Flint sent Wyatt away and divided up his wives and possessions amongst the men. Since Spencer had recently done the Prophet a weighted and sensitive favor I can't quite access the specifics of, the Prophet had given him first pick of the seven women, and Spencer had always had a bit of an eye for Taylee, so he couldn't bring himself to say no and ended up taking no small amount of flak from his first three for the next year, but he'd do it again if he had the chance. Her eyelashes damp from the sweat she wipes off her brow before setting the new can of ginger ale down on the nightstand is enough to soften and ease the tight terribleness in his gut.

—

The Prophet's youngest wife, Nephi, ate my ribs yesterday, licking the barbecue sauce they slathered me in off her fingers as she stared at the back of Wyatt Shumway's glossy black hair sticking out from beneath a baseball hat. She can't stop thinking about the way the man's shoulders slope gentle and smooth down from his long, elegant neck. All his lines unfurl into a resounding whole. Nephi's been lying in her bed, which smells like the Prophet's aftershave, all day, thinking about Wyatt's eyes beneath the shadow of the red baseball hat and listening to Sariah slam cabinets and scrape chairs against the floor as she hate-cleans the kitchen. The slamming's got something to do with some simmering strife between the Prophet's first three wives, Eliza and Sariah and Jossilyn, about who's going to host dinner on the final night of the festival. Shaylee, the sixth wife and Nephi's best friend, told Nephi something about it yesterday, but Nephi didn't pay much attention. She usually stays out of all the conversations the wives have about logistics and semantics. There's no point belittling herself in a desperate attempt to attain fleeting scraps of power from the other wives when she's stuffed full of more than she knows what to do with and has been ever since the Prophet announced to the congregation that he'd had a holy vision of Nephi in a white veil in the middle of the night.

—

For a moment, after Craig appeared inside the boy with me, I was wild with the thought of you joining me here soon, Ava. It was always our plan to go out together before our seventh year, the year we'd be taken to the festival. You'd rip my throat out with your teeth, then I'd rip your throat out with mine, and they'd never get the chance to hurt us, and we'd always be together. But then they came and took you to sow somewhere far away, and I couldn't stop them, I couldn't follow you, I couldn't find you. I wanted to fall to the floor, disappear beneath the weight of the herd. But I didn't want to let myself off the hook so easily. I figured the festival would serve as a penance for the failure I'd done you. That whole week and all I suffered—it'll never be enough.

—

Taylee Kimball ate my hock and jowls for dinner last night. She doesn't like the taste or texture of meat, and when she was married to Wyatt Shumway he let her keep a vegetarian diet, but her new husband says it's unhealthy to avoid meat, and makes her eat double what the other wives eat to make up for all those years she went without. Taylee could have gone with Wyatt when he left, and a part of her wanted to, but her parents and the children and her sisters and her soul and God. She begged Wyatt not to say anything about the voices, but he wouldn't listen to anything she said, said he knew what he was doing, said he had to do what he was doing—a matter of faith.

—

"What the hell is going on?" Nephi asks Shaylee as the girl comes into Nephi's bedroom and throws herself across the mattress. "It sounds like she's got the carpet cleaner out now."

"Sariah wants to cook in her kitchen on the last day of the festival," Shaylee explains, "but Jossilyn says Sariah's kitchen only has the one oven, plus she always uses too much salt, so they really ought to cook in her kitchen, which has the two ovens and is closer to the driveway and the truck and all the supplies that are going to need to be unloaded, and what a pain it would be to lug all those sacks of potatoes through Eliza's house, out into the backyard, past the pool, behind the garage, around the rosebush, and into Sariah's house."

"Unimaginative cows," Nephi says. Shaylee hands her a bowl full of cherries, and Nephi picks one up, puts it in her mouth. The cherry starts to sing the lyrics of that infectiously hypnotic song Sariah's younger brother's band played with bass and drums and screeching microphones on the wooden stage while I ran to the field behind the chokecherry to meet my body's end beneath the desert juniper.

Quiet, I tell the cherry. *I'm trying to hear this.* Much to my chagrin, the cherry continues to hum the song. Nephi rolls the cherry's pit between two fingers, tosses it on the nightstand. "I'm bored just thinking about their inner lives."

"I downloaded the first episode onto my brother's phone."

"Shut up." Nephi sits up straight and holds out her small, stained hand.

—

You always smelled fresh, like the grass of the farm you grew up on, despite the shit and piss of the pen. You said I smelled like light, like my ancestors must have been kings. There's never been a pig king, though. I never quite knew when you were lying, when you were telling the truth. I so much more than liked the hair on your pink, wet snout, the way it swayed like the fairy-tale trees in your wild stories as you breathed in and out beside me, hard skull crushing into mine, leaving a permanent indent deeper than any scar.

—

Wyatt Shumway got in late last night and walked through the festival with a hat pulled down over the top of his head. The bottom part of his head was covered with a new beard, and almost no one recognized him as he ordered a slice of my shoulder and sank into the meat like an old bed. You told me Pigasus, a 145-pound pink domestic pig, was nominated as president of the United States just before the Democratic National Convention in the year 1968 in the Chicago Civic Center right next to the Picasso. His campaign managers insisted he be given Secret Service protection and White House foreign policy debriefings. I smiled when you told me this story, and my small pink soul filled up with pride thinking of Pigasus flying up high like that with everyone cheering him on, but then you laughed, and I thought you'd made it up as a joke to be cruel like you sometimes were, but you shook your head and said no, Pigasus was the joke; his campaign managers paraded him around with a banner that read: IF WE CAN'T HAVE HIM IN THE WHITE HOUSE, WE CAN HAVE HIM FOR BREAKFAST. Wyatt is back in town to get his stuff, and since he's famous now the Prophet can't stop him.

—

When Bridger gets to the river, he doesn't find a chicken to throw at Ronan Young's fat face. He finds the dead and bloated body of Eliza Flint. The eggs he ate this morning shriek and fly away.

—

The Prophet comes into Nephi's room right after she hides the phone under her mattress. She thinks he didn't notice her quick, guilty movements, but it's hard to tell with him because his face never gives anything away. Unless he wants to, like when he looks at Shaylee and she leaves and shuts the door behind her. The cherry's no longer humming any pop songs. I'm alone, and it's very quiet inside the girl. The Prophet sits down on the bed next to Nephi and pulls out a box from his pocket. Ruby earrings. He takes them out of the box and puts them in her ears, delicately. She stands up and looks in the mirror. They glow, make her skin glow. Nephi's practicing how to never give anything away either. She's not as good as he is, but one day she will be.

"Do you like them?" he asks.

"Yes."

"Do you want me inside you?" he asks.

"Yes," she says. The back of her knees, whatever that space is called, is hot and full of sweat that itches like salt in a cut. And then, after: "Thank you."

She would like to go rinse off, but he makes her lie there with her feet up on the wall while he runs a finger over her belly and tells her their son will be his favorite, the one who inherits everything.

When he leaves, Nephi gets dressed and pulls her hair up to show off her ears. She goes downstairs and sits at the kitchen table until Sariah looks at her and sees the rubies. Then it's only a matter of time until all the other wives find out and feel jealous and ugly and unwanted. Nephi smiles and stands, stretches so they can all get a good look at her long, straight body—the body that's wanted and loved and cherished more than any of theirs will ever be again—but inside her I can hear something that sounds like the sounds we little piglets made when they took Mother away and placed us in the pen and we cried in the dark in the corner, alone and irredeemable.

—

Sheriff Spencer Kimball is in the bathroom on the toilet when his son Alvin knocks on the door and says Larue's on the phone from the station and it's something important. Spencer Kimball says he can't talk right now; he'll call him back. Alvin says Larue says it's important. Spencer Kimball says he can't talk right now; he'll call back. Alvin says Larue says there's a dead body down at the river. Spencer Kimball says he can't talk right now; he'll call back. Alvin says Larue says the dead body is Eliza Flint's. Spencer Kimball gets up off the toilet and runs down the hall, buttoning his pants up as he shouts for his keys.

(blackout)

SWINE & CHEER FESTIVAL: DAY 9

You always did love a good mystery, Ava. You always did say they were your favorite stories. Sookie Zabriskie didn't tell you many because she was only nine, so mostly you made them up, and then you asked me who done it, and I'd try to think through the mystery, but I could never find any answers, and you'd never give me any hints, and you'd never relent and help me out of the dark. Now here I am in the very middle of a mystery. If I can solve it, maybe you will come back to me. I'm a little less here in this shitty field where my blood is drying beneath the rising sun than I was yesterday, though, and I've only got five more days to go until I slip away entirely into some other place where I might not be able to think of the delicate part in your hooves and the way I always wanted to burrow myself into that space snout first so I could inhale the very filthiest parts of you.

—

Since the Prophet and the legal wives are at the station and have been all night, Nephi spends the scorching morning in bed with the phone Shaylee stole, watching the small screen play episodes of *The Bachelor* under the comforter where it's dark and airless and private. I've never seen television before, but you told me all about it, Ava, and it's every bit as enchanting and vapid as you always said. I wish we could have curled up on the couch together with little Sookie Zabriskie, who'd feed us popcorn and scratch behind our ears while we watched something elegant and inventive, maybe one of those old black-and-whites you were always whispering to me about late at night. But little Sookie Zabriskie is dead at the bottom of a well, and you're being injected with top-of-the-line semen three times a year so you can pump out piglets until you go mad enough to eat them before they can be sold off so someone else can eat them and they cull you away, and an eighth of my soul is inside Nephi, and Chris Harrison, a mind-bogglingly dull and dry human male with a smooth speaking voice and the essentially desexualized manner of a court eunuch, appears on the screen every now and then to narrate the plotline of the reality show and transition from commercial breaks back into the story.

"For the first time in *Bachelor* history," Chris Harrison says to the camera, "our bachelor has a direct line to God himself. Tonight, I'll sit down with Wyatt Shumway on the eve of his journey and talk about what he wants from his future wife."

———

Wyatt Shumway is in his old trailer, going through the boxes that his seven wives packed up and stacked in the shed out back. I don't know what he's looking for, but I do know he is in Hagoth's Cross and not with Chris Harrison.

———

On the screen in Nephi's room, Wyatt Shumway is now sitting down across from Chris Harrison, both men in identical armchairs, ankles crossed over knees, faces serious and ready to get down to some emotional business. This must have been shot before, Ava, like the mystery story you told me about the actress who was murdered on that locked set where she was filming a movie about an actress who gets murdered, which was a remake of a movie that had been shot decades ago and had featured an actress who had also gotten murdered. Was it the cameraman, Ava, or the jealous husband, or the understudy? Damn you, Ava, you never told me anything that mattered.

Chris Harrison looks over at this past version of Wyatt Shumway and says with gravity: "All this started when one of our *Bachelor* producers met you just outside of Salt Lake City while he was on a road trip."

"That's right," Wyatt says. They're sitting on wicker chairs near an outdoor pool lit up blue in the night. "I'd just been kicked out of my home, had my family and property stripped away, and I didn't know where to go or what to do."

"He saw you and knew America would fall in love with you."

"I'd never seen the show. Never seen any show, really. He invited me to come stay in the mansion, meet the bachelorette, Allison, compete for the rose, the chance to propose to her. Honestly, I didn't understand half of what he was talking about. But he had a car, and he offered to put me up at a hotel, buy my dinner. I literally couldn't afford to say no. That night I prayed, and God said I should do the show but warned me Allison and I wouldn't end up together."

"You sure didn't."

"No, she chose Ryan, which was fine. That was their path. I knew someone else was meant for me."

"And now there are twenty-five women waiting inside this mansion for the chance to meet you. How does it feel?"

"Like I'm right where God wants me to be."

—

Dallin Gubler goes over his finances in the office and works the space in his mouth between two molars that may or may not be harboring an infection. He doesn't want to spend a single second thinking about what happened to Eliza. They lived right next door to one another until she married Gideon and became too good for the son of a pig farmer. The Swine & Cheer Festival is where he makes most of his annual income (75 percent of which goes to the Prophet), but because of some Biblical numerology he doesn't quite understand, only seven-year-old pigs can be used during the two-week celebration, so he must plan many years in advance in order to keep the whole operation running smoothly on his end. Piglets take three months to ripen in the womb. In nature, sows wean their piglets at three months, then keep their piglets close by for the next few years. But weaning more piglets per sow significantly decreases certain production costs per piglet weaned, or at least that's what the note Dallin is reading suggests:

Consider:

If sow feed costs $0.13 per pound, 1 ton of feed per sow

per year equals: $260 per sow per year, then increased

sow production lowers piglet cost as follows:

22 piglets/sow/year=$11.82/piglet

25 piglets/sow/year=$10.40/piglet

30 piglets/sow/year=$8.67/piglet

Looking at these numbers, I realize that sweet week we got with Mother before she was taken away to isolation so her body would reset and the eggs inside her would ripen, ready again for the insertion, was a luxury Dallin Gubler bequeathed us from the inside of his own personal wallet. My soul warms for the man, and I find myself overwhelmed by his small kindness. I might cry if only I had any eyes left.

—

Bridger goes to summer school at the temple in the mornings. Greeks had to wash their bodies before entering holy ground if they saw a dead body. It's Tuesday, and on Tuesdays they always do worksheets no matter how much he and the other boys complain.

—

Taylee is not supposed to talk about her former husband, let alone think about him. But Spencer's been at the station dealing with the fallout from Eliza Flint all day, and the rest of the wives are at the festival selling jam made from bacon grease and the blackberries that grow down by the tire swing, so Taylee closes the blinds and turns on the television so the Youngs can't spy and punches in the security code with the remote that's all greasy from Spencer's fingers because he always eats in front of the screen and he never wipes anything down. The password is Spencer's birthday. It's the same code for his ATM card and his laptop and his voice mail. ABC is showing infomercials rather than *The Bachelor*, though, so Taylee locks the television back up and sits down at her husband's desk, logs onto his laptop, types in "Wyatt Shumway." It's even stranger than television, Ava. Millions of websites arise in a matter of seconds (0.36 to be exact). Taylee clicks on the first option, and an article appears out of the ether like an apparition.

—

Sariah is in the blistering and close waiting room with Jossilyn, Alma, Meredith, and Shaylee. Her arm is numb, and so are her fingers. She closes them and opens them, trying to reignite something she doesn't understand. Gideon is behind the walls with Sheriff Kimball and has been for hours. Sariah keeps forgetting why she's here, and then she remembers that Eliza is dead and has been dead for hours. There's something wrong with Sariah's mind. Skipping and tripping and cycling. She feels like she's been here before, drinking this specific brand of ginger ale out of a can exactly as cold as the one sweating in her hand, staring at a muted oil painting of a goat in a field with one horn longer than the other while she imagines Eliza's body facedown in the dirty river. Eliza hated baths, only ever showered. She wouldn't have wanted to wash up on the shore and lie there in the water like that. She'd have rather been found halfway buried in the desert if she had any choice in the matter, which I guess she probably didn't.

—

SEASON PREMIERE: *THE BACHELOR*

The Bachelorette made history last year when producers cast the first polygamist contestant on the show. Wyatt Shumway was eliminated from Allison's dramatic season, but not before the soft-spoken man with eyes bigger and brighter than the giant glassy orbs of Paul Newman, hair like black satin and velvet, and a professed and (arguably) verified ability to speak with God himself, captured the hearts of viewers nationwide. To continue to capitalize off Shumway's charm, producers announced him as the new lead on *The Bachelor* a few months back, and tonight he met twenty-five women, eliminated eight, and kissed three.

Dating so many women at once is a shock for most contestants, but Shumway's background makes him uniquely prepared to handle the pressures that come along with being the show's leading man: "I grew up in a world where this was normal," Shumway told Chris Harrison before the first Rose Ceremony. "My parents, uncles, grandparents—the whole community—I didn't know any different, any better. But now I'm out of that environment, and I see how corrupt and disgusting and misogynistic the whole system is. It just makes me so honored and humbled and excited to go on this journey, to meet all these amazing and beautiful women. But most of all I'm ready to find my one true soul mate, get married, and start a real life. I know my wife is here, and I know we're going to have a son once we get married."

Chris Harrison nods and smiles and says, "I've always got faith in this process, but you've got it on good authority, don't you?"

Shumway smiles the wide, innocent, joyful smile that made America collectively swoon, looks up at the Hollywood sky, and says, "Yes, Chris, I sure do have it on the *only* authority."

Taylee makes a sound like a choke or a laugh. I can't quite hear the difference, and inside she doesn't know what she's feeling or why—she's all awash in a thick parching blackness as she continues reading the article.

Speaking of children, *The Bachelor* franchise is the creation of Mike Fleiss and Lisa Levenson, which, if you do a little digging, makes perfect sense. Before striking television gold with *The Bachelor*, Mike Fleiss was working on sensational projects like *World's Scariest Police Shootouts; World's Wildest Websites; Wow! The Most Awesome Acts on Earth;* and *Shocking Behavior Caught on Tape, Parts 1 & 2.* Lisa Levenson, on the other hand, was working on soap operas like *General Hospital.* A match made in—

Taylee doesn't care about any of this, so she scrolls down to the comment section, head aching from the light and the incessant longing for more information from the screen, and she hopes the words of these strangers talking about the man she used to be married to will either cheer her up or at least tilt her attention away from herself.

SouthernBelle95 *3 days ago*
wow guys wow cant believe the chemistry between these two—died when he gave her the FIRST IMPRESSION ROSE calling it: he totally ends up with Serena in the end. soooo cute 4 real life i want someone to look at me like that *sigh*

Trami Nguyen *3 days ago*
This season looks really...Low budget porn but more roses and less body hair?

Rona Topaz *2 days ago*
not to be supa soft but oml I LOVE YOU WYATT <3

TalkinDuringTheMovie *1 day ago*
Serena will be runner up, and then lead on The Bachelorette next season. Guarantee she's already signed contracts and locked in. U realize this is fake, right?

MsKittenLover11 *1 day ago*
dang I wish I could be on this show I love this show I have the same Birthday as serena but I am 12 :D

Charlene *5 hours ago*
where all the asian contestants at? o now I remember there killin it in o that's right EVERYTHING and not waste time on stupid shit show like this garbage also stfu TDTM why u here if so fake get a life

Lauren W. *1 hour ago*
he sort of hot I guez but why is no one more concerned that this dude is supposedly talking to God? ha WTF he cray & not THAT hot to like balance it outz

TalkinDuringTheMovie *5 minutes ago*
fuck off and die Charlene and you spell it THEY'RE NOT THERE did you drop out of third grade or what

Brian Kain *1 minute ago*
this shit lame but id bang the redhead tho nice tits

—

Spencer wants to go home and take a long, cold shower, but he's busy at the station trying to ward off the state police from interfering. Hagoth's Cross is self-governing and always has been, but when something like this goes wrong, the rest of the world always seems to suddenly want to be involved. Best way to keep them out is to find a suspect. Usually it's almost always the husband, but Spencer knows it can't be Gideon. If it's not the husband, it's the mistress, but in this case there are no mistresses, just a bunch of additional wives, and it can't be any of them, either. Spencer makes a list of all the men in Hagoth's Cross that he could name guilty of murdering Eliza Flint without royally pissing Gideon off and underlines the most likely suspect:

Aaron Orson

Jared Porter

Layton Young

Isaiah Ashton

<u>Dallin Gubler</u>

Ammon Brighten

Jacob Taylor

Oakley Olsen

Beckette Sorensen

Elijah Reber

Joel Kunz

(blackout)

SWINE & CHEER FESTIVAL: DAY 10

Wyatt Shumway wants to get out of town as fast as he can, but he's looking for a pair of baby shoes that he cannot find. They're the shoes his own mother wrapped his two small feet in when he was an infant. They're not in any of the boxes in the hot shed with the tin roof he's been rooting around in all day. Part of him thinks Gideon came out and stole the shoes just to fuck with him, but there's no possible way Gideon could have known how much those shoes meant to him. If Gideon wanted to fuck with him, he would have just gotten rid of everything. Not everything except the shoes, though if Gideon did know how much the shoes meant it would have been the exact perfect way to fuck with him.

Wyatt smacks a hand across the dashboard of his car and then pulls off onto the side of the road and prays. Lots of people pray, but Wyatt does it different. Most people say what they've got to say and then they're done. Wyatt closes his eyes and whispers *I'm listening* in his head, and then he waits. The waiting is monstrously excruciating. I wait with him, and the silence is as insufferable as the waiting. I never knew anything about God until you came into the swine yard and told me about the seven days of limbo and the later place full of grass and natural light where nothing stinks like piss or shit and everything is full of God. I asked you what God was. You made most of it up, I think, but your words were always more real to me than anything else could ever be. I think Wyatt believes in a different sort of god than the one you spoke to me of. This god scares me, and I'm scared as I'm waiting with Wyatt, who's also scared but also feverishly expectant, electrified with anticipation.

—

Taylee's shoulders ache from hunching over the laptop screen, but she doesn't bother to stretch them out. She scrolls through a list of videos and then clicks on one where a blond girl in her early twenties who's so beautiful it's uncomfortable to even just look at her face through Taylee's eyes and a screen gazes into this side of the screen and moves her mouth, as if she's talking, but no noise comes out. Taylee adjusts the volume and the blond girl, who's labeled SERENA down in the left-hand corner of the screen, continues her soliloquy: "I think Wyatt is the perfect guy. Honestly, I feel like the luckiest girl in the world just to get the chance to come here tonight and meet him. Look at him—totally rocking the tall, dark, and handsome. And plus it's just so rare to meet a guy who's invested in commitment and loyalty. He wants to come out of this experience with a wife, so he can start a family. A real family, not like that polygamist cult he was raised in. And I think it's just so brave that he left that whole life behind to come here, and I'm so totally excited to start this adventure with, like, the man who's maybe my future husband."

—

Sariah cannot seem to get out of bed this sultry morning. The other wives have come in and out several times, offering iced water and asking questions and suggesting remedies, but Sariah cannot muster the energy to even acknowledge their presence. It's not that she's tired, or even particularly sad. The numbness has spread up, and she simply cannot get up out of bed.

The sun is coming in red and thick when Gideon knocks on the door and comes in. He sits on the bed next to her and rests a hand on her forehead. "It's not your fault," he says. Sariah curls away from him and cries into her pillow. She always hears people talk about how nice it is to have a good cry, how cleansing. She doesn't feel cleansed. Gideon lies down beside her and pulls her close to him, his hands digging into her ribs, and then he presses his face into the space between her shoulders, and after a while the thick cotton of her nightshirt starts to feel wet. He can't be crying, so she assumes she is dreaming.

—

Bridger Rigby has a butcher's knife in his hand and is running barefoot through the balmy meadow well ahead of the other boys after Randal. I hate Randal hard and heavy even in my new state, not for his fat ass and all the shit I ate from him over the years but because he was the pig on the other side of you, and I begrudged him for touching you when I wanted you to be only mine. He always kept to himself and never really got in the middle of our conversations, except to ask a clarifying question about one of your increasingly befuddling stories, which of course only served to make me look clever and more on your level than anyone else could ever possibly be, so perhaps I should have loved him a little, as a member of my herd, a brother, but I didn't ever love him, Ava, I was never as good as I should have been, and still I'm full of hate, so it gives me no small pleasure to watch his legs run fast as they can but not fast enough. I know just what it feels like to be the pig that gets knocked down and tied up and sliced into, but I must say I much prefer to be the boy with the knife chasing the pig down, blood pumping through his full vibrating veins like thunder as the thrill of the chase bleeds into the thrill of victory and he leaps onto Randal and my rhapsodic pink soul cheers him on as he shoves his knife into Randal's belly until he feels a give like a broken orange peel and the hot wet red pours out all over all of us.

—

Being inside Dallin Gubler is like being inside a dark bar full of cigarette smoke and the smell of vomit at ten in the morning. He stands outside the scorching ring where the Pig Catching Contest is happening and watches as the writhing pigs are brought out into the arena in burlap sacks and dumped into the dirt, where they immediately start running quick as their little pink legs can run. It usually only takes a few laps for the pigs to realize that they're in an enclosed stadium and there's no hope of escape or fight or salvation. Still, something keeps them all running. Something kept me breathing and eating and shitting in the pen even without you, Ava, and it wasn't penance like I want it to have been. It wasn't the will to live or anything glorious like how I know you'd try to spin it.

A boy grabs a frightened pig and wrenches him into a burlap sack with the help of a woman who is probably his mother. "How barbaric," a passing lady mutters under her breath.

"You oughta see what happens after the chase." Dallin laughs, then steps into the ring for his turn. He catches and bags his pig within seven seconds, and the crowd cheers.

—

Nephi is under her bed watching another episode of Wyatt's season of *The Bachelor*. His cheekbones are immaculately sculpted as if by some divine force, and her whole baking body physically hurts when she looks at his image on the screen from wanting and not being able to have, like a magnet denied its very magnetism, but still she cannot look away from the screen. A Date Card delivered by some mysterious off-camera force arrives at the house full of women in their twenties with perfect hair and white teeth and beautiful clothes and loving supportive families that are not members of ridiculous humiliating cults, and tags down in the left-hand corner of the screen under their cute perky names inform the viewer of their occupations, each more glamorous than the last: flight attendant, cruise ship singer, real estate agent, personal trainer, dog rescuer, blogger, dental hygienist.

The real estate agent opens up the Date Card and reads a single word: "Kristen." All the women scream, and the camera zooms in on the cruise ship singer. The real estate agent finishes reading the Date Card: "Are you ready to trust your heart and fall?" All the women scream again, and the cruise ship singer says, "Oh my God. Do you think we're bungee jumping?" and looks around at the other women in fear, but they shake their heads and shrug and say they don't know.

A limo pulls up, and the cruise ship singer gets into the limo with Wyatt, and he says, "I hope you're not afraid of heights," and she says, "I'm very much afraid of heights," and they both laugh, and Nephi wants to cry because the whole thing is so damn romantic. Wyatt looks at the cruise ship singer and says, "I'm looking for someone to be my wife. But I'm also looking for someone to be the mother of my child. And God told me that the mother of my child is a brave woman who faces her fears, and that's who I'm looking for, because God's never steered me wrong so far."

—

Spencer Kimball walks through downtown's blistering asphalt streets with his handcuffs in the back pocket of his jeans looking for Dallin Gubler. He finds him on a corner wearing a sash across his overalls, drinking a Pepsi from a brown paper bag. "Come with me," Spencer says. "You're in a whole heap of trouble."

—

Bridger Rigby takes a bite of Randal, and I must admit I've never tasted anything quite so spectacular as the crackling rays of salted fat of his loins peppered by the exalted fear he felt as the boys brought out the wrenches and got to work on his face before Bridger slit his throat and cut him up over the bonfire. Maybe I was afraid to die, Ava, and so I didn't fall to the floor and stop eating even after you were gone. Maybe I'm a coward. *Is that you, Amos Throckmorten?* Randal asks. *Where am I? Who's this boy? Is it over?*

—

Wyatt's pulled over on the side of the road in the oven-roasting car, still listening for the voice of God. It takes a long time, sometimes. God's not anyone's bitch, and he's got a lot of shit to take care of. Wyatt waits patiently. I wait, but I'm not so patient. I want to hear God, and I want it bad even though I'm just a lowly little pig with no right to hear anything divine or majestic. If God's really real like you said, Ava, then we'll be together again somewhere maybe. And if I could just somehow know for certain—*Amos Throckmorten III.* The voice sounds like it's coming from a giant down deep inside a well. *That's right. It's me, Amos. The one true God. I've come here to tell you that you're the most shit-eating asshole of all the shiteating assholes on the planet.*

There's laughter, and then: *Just fucking with you, dude, it's me, Craig. Got you, didn't I? Didn't I? Oh man, I so did. You totally thought I was God. You totally—Amos? Come on, man, don't be like that. It's just a joke, for Christ's sake. Have a sense of humor, you sallow sonofabitch.*

(blackout)

SWINE & CHEER FESTIVAL: DAY 11

The grocery store's fluorescent lights are harsh on Taylee's eyes after so much time spent in her bedroom gazing at the screen. She feels as if she's somehow already grown unaccustomed to gazing at anything three-dimensional and more than three feet away from her face, which feels stiff and pale and doesn't know how to look at people anymore. It's so nice to look at people and have them not be able to look back at you. It's probably the single best thing Taylee's ever experienced in her life, and I can't really argue with her on that point. I can feel my soul fading away from this world and these people who ate me, but I'm not ready to go and leave them to their own fates without me; I'm not ready to go away and be me without them or you or my herd or my body. I don't know what that me looks like, feels like, and, Ava, I'm afraid; Ava, I'm a coward.

Jossilyn Flint emerges at the end of the bread aisle and makes her way toward Taylee. "I'm so sorry for your loss," Taylee says because that's what she's supposed to say. "Thank you," Jossilyn Flint says, and then she stands there and looks at Taylee. Taylee doesn't know what else she is supposed to say or do. "Spencer says he arrested Dallin Gubler last night." As soon as the sentence is out, it seems like a bad idea to have spoken it, but Jossilyn doesn't get upset. She nods and says, "Yes, and perhaps now Sariah will come to her senses."

—

Nephi puts on her rubies and walks down the hall languidly, running her fingers along the drywall. She finds Shaylee in the kitchen, kneading dough for another pie. Nephi sits down across from her and watches her work. "Let's go down to the festival," Nephi says. "We can't go without Gideon," Shaylee says. "I want to see if Wyatt's still in town," Nephi says. "What's that matter to you?" Shaylee asks. "I'm going to tell him I want to run away with him," Nephi says. "You're crazy," Shaylee says. "I'll sell these rubies, and we'll start a new life," Nephi says. "He's already got a new life," Shaylee says. "He's only back in town to get his things, and then he's off to marry Serena, and they won't need to sell any jewelry because she's a dental hygienist." Nephi picks up a fistful of dough and throws it at Shaylee, then stands up, pats her dress down, and walks back up to her room, her blood crackling.

—

Wyatt goes to the post office and picks up a package sent from his fiancée. Lately she's only been eating farm-to-table, humanely raised meat, and she wants him to do the same. When he told her that he didn't see why he should, she begged him to just try a cut of steak and see if it wasn't the best thing he'd ever tasted. "When there's no fear or anxiety in the animal, the meat's so much fresher. It's like sinking your teeth into a fat, juicy cloud." He opens the package and takes out a cut of beef jerky, bites into it.

Hello? I say, curious about this fellow and this "humane" farm he hails from.

Who's that? Where am I? What's happening? Oh God dear God help me God.

Whoa, whoa. Calm down, man. We're only dead.

So it's over, then?

That's right. Well, almost. This is sort of the last act.

Thank the heavens.

Did they torture you, too? For the taste?

No, no, of course not. She wanted us calm. For the taste. She'd come out and pet us and give us carrots and talk cute sweet baby talk like who's a precious little moo cow darling to us like she loved us, but every few days more and more of us would disappear. We all knew what was happening, and we all knew it was only a matter of time before—but I always sort of hoped, you know. Maybe she'll love me more. Maybe she'll look into my big black eyes and I'll flutter my eyelashes and she'll love me so much she won't be able to kill me and cut me up and eat me.

But alas.

But alas little moo cow darling is dead.

—

Sariah sits beside her husband as he drives her to the temple. Something is very wrong with her. She's always doing bad things and then feeling bad about the bad things and then promising to never do the bad things again and then doing the bad things again and again and again. It's torture to be inside a body with conflicting voices and ideals. It's insane to do the same thing over and over again despite not ever wanting to do the thing ever again, despite never wanting to do it in the first place. "Pray," he tells her. "When you get the urge, just pray. It's virtually impossible to sin and pray at the same time. It works for me, sometimes." She looks at his profile like she's seeing it for the first time. "And other times?" He shrugs his shoulder, looks out at the road. *Thank thee for this day. Thank thee for all our many blessings. Thank thee for this day. Thank thee for all our many blessings. Thank thee for this day. Thank thee for all our many blessings.*

—

Bridger Rigby's sweatshirt smells like the bonfire from last night, and the smoky smell reminds him of the time at the river when his uncle took him and his father out to prove God was talking straight to him. Uncle Wyatt loved the river and had a favorite spot he used to take Bridger down to fish at every summer. The three of them went down to the river that last time, and Uncle Wyatt took off his shirt and rolled up his jeans and waded a few feet out into the river and looked up at the sky and whispered something and the water around him parted like butter and he ran to the other side of the shore without even getting a bit of his jeans wet. He came back to the other side of the shore and pointed up at a nearby mountain and said, "See that mountain there? I'll have God move it over there to the west if you still don't believe me." But Bridger and his father shook their heads and cried and said no, please, stop, no more, please, let's all just go home, please, we're sorry.

—

Dallin's temporary holding cell is small and sultry and has a window facing out toward downtown, where the festival is still going strong despite the week's theatrics. He can smell pork sizzling over a fire. When his mouth starts to water, I feel the tingling desire in my soul like an itch I'm scratching and wanting to scratch at the same time.

—

Spencer Kimball meets the Prophet Gideon Flint outside the temple, and together the two men walk through downtown. "Did he really do it?" the Prophet asks. "We'll get a confession soon enough," Spencer Kimball says, and then he stops at a vendor who's selling pigs' feet on a stick. "My treat," he offers, but the Prophet shakes his head and says, "I don't eat meat," which is a shame because I would love to be inside his opaque head.

(blackout)

SWINE & CHEER FESTIVAL: DAY 12

Bridger Rigby is sick, vomiting every three to seven minutes. He's given up even trying to return to his bed and instead has staked out a nice comfortable spot on the blissfully cool bathroom tile. In between dry heaving sour nothing into the pungent toilet bowl, he thinks about how his Uncle Wyatt most certainly has a direct line to God but how this conflicts with what he's always been taught at temple, that only the one true Prophet can speak with God, and so is it possible that Gideon is a fraud and not a true prophet, seeing as how he's never put forth any, like, certifiable proof of his relationship with God, and but so then is it possible that Gideon killed Mrs. Eliza, who always saved Bridger a piece of her lemon cake on holidays because she knew it was his favorite and there was that one year in second grade when he didn't get any during Christmas and she smiled and said, "Next time," and he smiled back and nodded his head like his heart wasn't breaking.

—

On a website dedicated to the blossoming relationship between Serena and Wyatt, Taylee stumbles across a chat forum that's dedicated to some prophecy about the new couple's future child.

TheEverlastingBobStopper *3 days ago*
WS says he wanted to go on the show in order to find a wife, but all he ever talks about is the future-son he's going to have with the future-wife...poor girl :(

ConspiracyLife94 *3 days ago*
God gave him a prophecy remember? WS talks about it in one of those interviews with CH before the season started off. The son he has with the winner is supposed to bring about the salvation of mankind. The whole reason he's doing the show is to create the child, save mankind, bring harmony to the universe, etc.

PineAppleZZZ *3 days ago*
Really ups the stakes this season.

CharmagneReigning *3 days ago*
I don't normally go in for this sort of thing, but honestly if WS and Serena had a baby I have zero doubt it would somehow be capable of saving mankind just based on genetic good looks alone.

EliRoseDeLaCerna *3 days ago*
There are so many forces working against the birth of this child, but good will prevail that flight attendant is a skank getting sent home without a rose soon praise in the name of jesus christ AMEN

Taylee feels hollow inside where her four children used to dream. She picks up a box of candies and pops a few in her mouth. I listen to the sweets chat to one another about the state of the pound versus the euro as Taylee puts her new husband's laptop away so he won't know what she was up to while he was away at work, although there's a very real part of her that wants to leave the laptop up where he can see just where her mind's been lately, not because she wants to get caught but because she's so exhausted from being alone.

—

Sariah tries to pray like Gideon told her but all she can see is Eliza and all she can think of is all the horrible things she ever thought about her and all she can do is imagine that all her red vicious thoughts somehow conjured this fate for the woman who washed her hair after she severed a vertebra giving birth to their fourth daughter.

—

Wyatt steps away from his agent, who's come all the way out here to talk to him about an interview she wants him to do that will supposedly be life changing. I want to hear him talk to God, see if it's real, but I can't hold on much longer, and he can't pray when there are so many people around. He answers his phone and says hello to his fiancée. She asks him how the beef jerky was, and he says that he's had better. He asks her why she ever went and signed up for the show in the first place. She says that she just felt so overwhelmed with all the different ways her life could go, like she was standing atop this vast, endless, infinite sea. She liked the idea of signing up for something nice and formulaic, something with a beginning and a middle and an end, something with definite villains and definite heroes and a happily ending marriage that ties up all the loose strings and erases the past with a $100,000 ring.

—

Dallin lies in his humid cell on the cot and looks up at the ceiling. Shadows from outside his window play on the plaster, reminding him of Eliza and the way she'd smile when he made that stupid dog shadow puppet on his wall that she could see from behind the window of her pink bedroom.

—

Since Gideon is gone, Nephi sneaks out of the house and heads to the festival, hoping to casually run into Wyatt. She sees him standing by the cotton candy cart, but when she reaches out a hand to tap his shoulder the woman standing next to him grabs her and gazes intently at the wedding ring Gideon gave her a few months back. "Oh God, Wyatt," the woman says. "Is this one of those poor polygamist girls you were telling me about? She's so young. Much too young for a wedding ring. Are you okay, sweetheart? Do you want me to call the police?" Nephi pushes her hair back so the rubies show. "My husband is the one true Prophet, and I don't need anything from anyone."

—

Spencer Kimball wipes the sweat off his forehead with his red bandana, stuffs it in his back pocket, and then steps up to the podium. "Ladies and gentlemen," he says. "It is with much pride that I announce the sinning culprit responsible for this most tragic and untimely death has been apprehended and is being held until further notice."

(blackout)

SWINE & CHEER FESTIVAL: DAY 13

Bridger Rigby sits at a picnic table downtown with his friends as they pass a bucket of lard around, dipping their fingers in and sucking.

"What do you call a pig that can tell you about his ancestors?"

"History in the bacon."

"What do you call a cow with no legs?"

"Ground beef."

"Why did the pig go into the kitchen?"

"He felt like bacon."

"What did the farmer say when he lost one of his cows?"

"What a miss-steak."

"What would happen if pigs could fly?"

"The price of bacon would skyrocket."

—

Thank thee for this day. Thank thee for all our many blessings.
Thank thee for this day. Thank thee for all our many blessings.
Thank thee for this day. Thank thee for all our many blessings.
Thank thee for this day. Thank thee for all our many blessings.
Thank thee for this day. Thank thee for all our many blessings.
Thank thee for this day. Thank thee for all our many blessings.
Thank thee for this day. Thank thee for all our many blessings.
Thank thee for this day. Thank thee for all our many blessings.

—

On screen, Wyatt asks Serena if she will accept his rose. Serena says yes and smiles so wide it seems her face might crack straight open. Nephi sticks her face in her pillow and screams so hard something snaps in her throat.

—

Outside the jail cell, the townspeople gather and chant and throw rotten fruit up at the window where Dallin looks out and down, thinking of Joseph Smith, who had a holy vision and wound up in jail for treason and conspiracy in 1844 before a furious mob dead set against polygamy stormed into the cell and murdered him and his brother. The martyring worked out well in the long run, but Dallin doesn't like pain.

—

Taylee looks down at the pair of baby's shoes she's got sitting on the passenger seat. The radio plays songs that she's not supposed to listen to, but she turns it up and listens anyway, just like she always does, sings along to that same song the cherries were singing inside Nephi. I've never heard music before all this, Ava, and I don't know what all the fuss is about. I wish I could hear just half a moment of your voice. Say anything, I don't care—sing this stupid song if you want, just don't leave me alone here fading into nothing without you coming into the nothing with me.

Taylee picks up the shoes and throws them out the window. They twist and spin in the rearview mirror before coming to a tangled stop in the mirage's shadow as a commercial for a mattress company begins with a catchy jingle.

—

Spencer Kimball can hear the mob from his desk. He thinks Dallin Gubler is maybe guilty, but he doesn't feel it in his gut viscerally the way he likes to when a case is done and over.

—

My blood is nearly gone from the field behind the chokecherry, beneath the desert juniper. I still don't know who killed Eliza Flint, and maybe I never will. Maybe it was Gideon. I think he must be fairly shitty inside. Dallin and Wyatt and Sariah and all the rest—they're all shitty inside, but maybe we're all a little shitty inside, even me, Ava, even you, high up on the pedestal I've placed you on, all the better to gaze shittily upon your sweet pink form—the way you always hogged the slop and laughed when describing Mrs. Zabriskie's face when she looked down in the well and saw Sookie's twisted neck and sometimes cut me off mid-sentence and ignored me when I talked like you just wanted me there as an ear, not a pig with a mind and a heart and a small pink soul corrupt as all the rest—and who's to say what's worse and what's redeemable and what's unforgivable and what might as well just be tossed in the trash and forgotten about and what's recoverable and what's salvageable and what's lost and hopeless and irredeemable, so maybe we should just say goodbye to the idea that anything or anyone should ever be clean and shitless, Ava, instead of standing still and judging and shitting more shit all over this big twirling rotating orb of a shitpile, but I can't move on without you no matter how shitty you were—maybe the best and only thing I could ever do is stand in the shit and smell the shit and roll in the shit and true love the shit despite its shittiness and because of its shittiness, our shittiness, our eternal unremarkably hallowed shittiness.

—

Wyatt pulls over on the side of the road and says, *I'm listening.* The last time he tried this, he didn't ever hear back, but he doesn't let that bother him. There's no fear in his heart, no wobbling doubt that what he believes might not be real and tangible. I envy him that, Ava. I sometimes question whether or not you were ever a real pig standing pressed up against me or if you were always only just a piece of my imagination.

Wyatt closes his eyes, and a voice that's not mine or Craig's or Randal's, a voice that doesn't belong to anything earthly or typical or anemic, rings out like a bell in a cathedral: *Take Highway 73 down to the old tollbooth and pull off on the side before the three-quarter-mile marker.* My pink soul trembles. Wyatt does just as the voice tells him to do, and then he gets out of his car and finds the pair of baby shoes he was looking for all along.

(blackout)

SWINE & CHEER FESTIVAL: DAY 14

Bridger Rigby has decided to stay home even though the final day of the festival is the peak of the celebration. It's the day that the festival's Big Pig is sacrificed on the scaffold in the middle of downtown. Cornelius's hair has been shaved into patterns, and his skin has been stretched across a metal frame that is now being paraded on a float through the streets along with his roasting body. A pineapple has been stuffed into his slack mouth, and slices of Cornelius are being cut off and handed to the highest bidders. Sariah throws a handful of cash at the vendor and takes a bite of the simmering meat. It tastes gritty, like sand, and she spits it out on the sizzling asphalt before joining the mob marching viciously toward the jail cell where Dallin Gubler is sitting on his cot, looking up at the ceiling and waiting for the mob with as much dignity as his shaking body will allow him. Spencer Kimball has gone home because his first wife called and told him that Taylee is missing, just like Nephi, who felt something stir in her belly early this morning and ran out to the river to think about Wyatt, who's hearing the voice of God telling him to do something absurd and unconscionable again, but I'm gone before I understand—gone to the field behind the chokecherry, beneath the desert juniper where I thought I'd be alone for a time with my thoughts and with you before I left this place for good and ever, but the Prophet is walking alone through the field, and I'd give almost anything to know what he's thinking as he puts his hands in his jacket pockets and pivots.

(whiteout)

Brothers

Charlene Logan

Two dogs wait at the edge of the forest. The sable-head one gnaws a pine cone. His plumed tail thumps the parched ground. His sidekick, a pepper-coat collie, stands at attention, eyeing the occasional car or truck that slows, the drivers thinking *coyotes* but realizing *dogs*. Two dogs. Where'd they come from?

It's dusk, and the road is flanked by sugar pine and yearling white fir. What is left of the day flattens. The dogs curl together. Brothers, they are used to keeping each other warm.

Shifting gears, the last logger out of the forest spots the dogs in the shine of his headlights. The pepper-color one sits upright. The other yips, wags his tail. The logger considers pulling over, but it is late, and he has a long drive. He thinks of them, though, when he stops at the nearest diner and asks the waitress, "What were they doing out there?"

She pours coffee. "The economy. People just dump them."

He thinks maybe he should go back. He had a collie once, a good dog. But he needs to keep moving. It's his livelihood. Someone else will stop.

The waitress hears of two more sightings. An older couple sits at the counter and orders apple pie. They were driving the upper mountain backroads in search of wildflowers—redbud shrubs, waterfall buttercups, the rare wild orchid. "Craziest thing. Two dogs blocked the road. So dirty, our first thought was wolves."

The waitress thinks about driving out to feed them, bathe them, find them good homes. She soon forgets, and only one dog is now spotted. The sable-head. The little boy eating ice cream at the counter mimics the dog's crazed eyes, lolling tongue, as he chased his family's car. "My mom said it had rabies."

On her first free day, which is weeks later, the waitress packs deli meat and bread and drives out to where the dogs were last seen. She whistles. Pokes around in the brush. She finds them. Curled against each other. The brothers' bodies sunk into the ground like deadfall.

The Ass of Otranto

Marilyn Moriarty

Was this a kneeling holy day, like the Friday that's Good, good for those who can loaf, though it's a bad time for sheep when fasting stops at Easter? The long fast makes men eager for midnight when the Big Lamb wakes and they slaughter the little ones.

Enzo decorated me with ashes under the wisteria vines by the firepit. He filled both hands with ashes from the cold fire and rubbed them all over me, darkened even my face, and striped my legs with his dirty hands. I smelled like smoke. He wore a hat. I rubbed my face against his shirt. He rubbed my chin. "Let's go," he said.

We went to a stripped field where an old oak leaned against air into nothing. The day felt like winter though it was not. Even the birds had fled. A tuft of hair like thistledown remained from a hawk's last meal. It is always dangerous when people meet and there is only one ass in the neighborhood. If anything has to be carried, dragged, or pulled, it's the animal who's tagged for it, especially when you've been specially decorated for the occasion.

The man who was married to Santa Maria from the

Christmas pageant came, keeping his hands folded up inside his sleeves. He sat on a gnarled tree root. I can bear a heavy weight if it is balanced, but that fat pumpkin leaned this way and that way. My right foreleg on the step, she fell back to the left. Left hind leg went up, she lurched to the right. My back swung like a rope bridge crossed by an army. Why didn't she set her feet down and give her weight to the stones? My heart beat faster than cricket legs. I could have carried her, I know, if she sat in time with the sway my steps put in her back. When I fell, my knees became walnuts cracking on the steps of the duomo. Santa Maria crashed to the ground like the tomatoes the boys throw at my feet.

Stephania came, with her runtlings. Some monks, more than four, and some men from the village. Paolo was there, too, newly washed, with clothes that smelled of the rocks in the river. I wondered if he would beat me or twist my lip as he always did, but all he did was talk.

Paolo said to the monks, "The criminal is now here."

I looked around for the culprit but saw no stranger there.

Enzo sat on a rock and folded his hands.

"Let the trial begin," Father Malaterra said. "The charge is murder. Murder of Father Antipater."

The monk with his arm around one of Stephania's runtlings spoke. "Father Antipater was beloved of us. He gave us the sacrament for many years. His hair was white, but his beard was not. He gave himself penance at night. He never knew a woman. Now he has been murdered. His murderer must pay. An eye for an eye. *Lex talionis.*"

My ears turned like sails toward the runtling. Did he think I forgot? At the end of a day when Enzo hired me out to Stephania to carry wood to market, her runtling gave me a bite of an apple and threw the rest in a water trough. Water flooded my nostrils and eyes when I plunged into the trough after it. "You can drown an ass in a water trough!" The boy thought this was a great joke.

One man said, "It's not right, not right that he died, not right at all."

Another said, "No. It's not." The man next to him looked at my master for help.

This man was our neighbor. I never saw him up close before, but he stole cabbages from our field at night. Was this the murderer, bony as a war horse? Was I supposed to carry him to the gallows? That's the good thing about war; it made everyone around here skinny. It would be hard to hang a thin man. Light as laundry, he might blow away on the wind. For sure, they would have to pull down on his ankles.

My skin twitched. Dust baths are good, and I wanted one. These ashes clogged up my nostrils. If I opened my mouth, my spit would drop out and take some of the ashes on my chin with it.

"Who will speak for him?" Father Malaterra asked.

The champion was my master, old Enzo. No colt kick in his legs.

"Sometimes, accidents happen. Even to good men. It was an accident."

Father Malaterra's nostrils flared. "Accidents?" he asked, his voice shrill. "Not a sparrow falls but God knows it. God allows no accidents. Everything is his will."

"I am simple man," Enzo said. "Maybe it was his will that our dear beloved Father Antipater should come to heaven. The ass is only an animal. He cannot make decisions. He reacted to the priest."

"He was a priest," Paolo said. "Who attacks a priest? Only evil attacks good."

Paolo, Enzo's nephew, prays all the time. He prays the Virgin will never appear to him. As a small boy, he trembled in his bed fearing that she would look in on him by moonlight.

"I will fast for twenty days before Lent," he told God. "Not even fish. Only onions."

Entreaties, rosaries, candles, masses, fasting—all this keeps her at bay. No wonder he is so foul-tempered; his religion makes him miserable. How could he forget the threat of her? Everywhere you look, there is an advertisement for God or his mother or his saints. One day the Virgin Mary will come to him and say, "My son, you spend too much time with whores."

Father Malaterra, presiding, said, "Augustine has written: Animals have no will. But they may be used by Satan because they were instruments. Then it is not wrong to punish Satan in them."

You'd think he would be talking about Paolo, but now it was animals. The ashes made my eyes tear up, and I blinked away drops.

Finally I understood. My own master had walked me into the barbecue to grill me like one of the saints.

"Who saw the ass strike Father Antipater?" Enzo asked, looking around, but no one did. They were only idiots, not perjurers.

One monk said, "Flight is the sign of guilt."

"It is the sign of fear," Enzo said. "But, in battle, a man may escape death if his horse flees. This ass has the horse in him."

"Uncle, he has the devil in him," Paolo said. "Many a man will die if the horse runs away from the man. I have prayed for all my life to the Santa Maria, the Blessed Virgin mother of God. She put the desire for prayer in my heart. But your beast keeps her away. I had a dream. Santa Maria said she cannot come when Otranto makes homely a place for Satan."

Enzo shook his head.

Tell them, I urged my master without words. He knew what Paolo was, but he said nothing for me against his kin.

"Who saw this?" Enzo asked again.

"We washed the body," a monk said. "There was a purple mark on his chest."

Enzo said, "Father Antipater was my soul's comfort. My living comes from my ass. Before you take my beast, which has served me, and carried wood for Stephania, and carried the Virgin in the pageant, who has no sin except he is small and cannot carry the burdens we pile on him, who falls, like Christ did, under the cross, before you take him, tell me the size of this mark. Tell me where it was."

"My fist. It was the size of my fist." The monk touched his chest. "The color was muddy. Red wine and dirt."

The monk had touched his own heart. Did I remember kicking the priest? Something firm met my hooves in the air. Where were soldiers when you needed them? A knight could testify to a death blow, but no monk here ever mounted a charger. Small flies came to drink water from my eyes, so I locked them shut for a second.

"He's too small," Enzo said.

"The devil," said Paolo.

"I was there," Enzo said. "I did not see the devil. Everything startles this animal. We have to cover his eyes to walk down the street. You know that."

"The animal is in us, and Satan is in the animal."

"Wash your hands, Paolo. Wash your feet. Take your clothes to the river. Wash your shitty ass on the leaves. The stink of the animal is on all of us."

Paolo said, "Uncle, I am surprised at you. You loved Father Antipater."

"You all are young. This priest heard your confessions—all of you. He was not murdered. If he was murdered, it was murder by death."

"The crazy woman—she attacked me. What is this world when the woman strikes the man and the ass kicks the priest?"

Enzo's shadow shrunk on the ground as the sun came to its point, but still he spoke. "All her children died. Her husband never came back."

"No," said the fat Madonna from the Christmas pageant. "No. No. My children are dead. Two. I gave them to God, where they rest in his bosom. We all weep for the men we lose on the sea. Or in war. But they serve God. We know this. Am I sad? Do I sit by the gate and curse strangers? I do not. I gave my children to God."

Many muttered. Did they agree or disagree? I couldn't tell. It sounded like the bleating of sheep to me. There was no shade here at all, and only one lousy tree. I don't know how they were going to hang anything from its rotten branches. After that, no one had anything else to say.

I stretched my back to piss. My dong dropped like a drawbridge. The steaming pool made froth in the dust.

The runtling pointed at me. "Mama, mama," the boy said now. "Look at that."

Foul runtling, bepiss yourself.

"Shut up, you." Stephania smacked him on the face. "It's just an animal."

Father Malaterra said, "The jury will now decide."

He took an old pot, broke it on a rock, and gave a fragment to everyone on the jury. "Make a mark," he said. "If you think he is guilty, make a mark. If he is innocent, don't do anything. Make no mark."

They did not give a piece to Enzo. It took two hands to write *guilty* but nothing to say *innocent*, and it looked like everyone made a mark. They handed their pieces to Father Malaterra when they were done.

Father Malaterra did not read them out one at a time but summed them together.

"It is decided," he said. "Guilty. He is guilty of murder. The ass is the devil's instrument. *Deo dandum*. We will give him to God. We will send a message to hell, saying Satan cannot live in the animals."

Enzo came to scratch my head.

Before Father Malaterra could take the rope from him, we saw a man in the distance kicking at the sides of a mule. The mule cantered, then trotted and walked before he trotted again. He was in no hurry, and who could blame him? Already the day was dry as sin. "Hey, hey!" the man shouted. "She's here, she's here. She came."

"*She's* here?" Father Malaterra said.

"*She's* here!" Paolo exclaimed, dropping to his knees.

"She's here!" the two-child-dead Madonna exclaimed. Her husband squeezed her arm.

"Yes. Finally. The German princess. The mayor made a holiday. Three days! What are you doing?"

Father Malaterra held the last shard in his hand.

"Father Antipater was murdered by the donkey. We are going to hang him. The court has decided it."

By now the man and his mule were within speaking distance. The mule turned nervously in his own circle. His ears asked, "What's up?" but I just flicked my tail.

"You can't do it today or tomorrow or for three days," the man said. "The mayor has declared a holiday, and the royals want to eat."

"But justice cannot wait," Father Malaterra said. "A murder was committed."

"Not today," the man said.

Paolo rose hastily and dusted off his hose.

"Don't be stupid," the man said. "Only pigs are murderers. Come into town. There is going to be a feast tonight."

Already I could see the mule rehearsing the tale he would take into town. *You should have seen the murderer they were going to hang. It was the rude pipsqueak. He sure looked relieved when we got there. Five more minutes, and it would have been over for the chump. One more after that, and his head would have been posted on the parapet, and the poor would be dining out.*

You'd think they were going to a funeral for God the way they left for home, disappointed because they had come for a hanging and there was none. Where were they going to do it? Not in this stinking field.

"You heard him," Enzo said to his nephew.

"What a day," was all he said as we walked home.

The way home always seems short, especially when you know at the end of the road is a spring of cool water and some new shoots the goats missed. The rest of the day was spoiled for any work. Enzo drew a pail of water and dumped the whole thing over me. The ashes made a gray slop slipping into the dust, and small flies drank at my fetlocks. He wiped down my back and legs with a clump of leaves. Even though we had walked on a smooth road, he lifted each hoof. *It's me*, my head said, butting his shoulder. Maybe he was checking to see if he got the right ass back, came home with the same animal he left with. At the end of a day, he touches his tools to count them. As he wiped down my damp neck, I felt his weight against my side. I gave him his weight back again. *Hello, fly*: My wet tail smacked his pants. He put one arm around me, as if he were going to hang his weight there. His chest felt warm. *You took me to the barbecue pit*: My tail spoke again. He leaned into me, stretching his chest against the length of my neck. I pushed my shoulder into his chest and gave my weight to that leg, leaning into him. He pressed an instant before he yielded and stepped back. I followed him with my weight. Little by little, we turned a slow circle backward. When he put his hand to my mouth, it smelled like fresh leaves, but I knew there would be nothing in it.

The Curious Case of the Cave Salamander

Gwen C. Katz

"The good news is, you're famous. The bad news is, the headline will grind your gears."

"And good morning to you, too, Kira," said Jen, acting casual to cover how much she wanted to grab Kira's phone and read the headline. "You're looking cute."

"I always look cute," said Kira. Neither the word *he* nor the word *she* had ever quite fit Kira, who preferred to go by *they*. Today they were wearing a yellow sundress and cherry lip gloss.

"Then it's ipso facto true today. What are the damages?" asked Jen. She sat at the kitchen table in her sweatpants, eating breakfast with Kira's daughter, Madison. As Kira set their phone on the table among the bowls and cereal boxes, Jen couldn't suppress a grin. A quote in the *New York Times* was a big deal, even if it was only a news brief.

The headline read, "Northwestern University Research Team Discovers New Species of Cave Salamander."

"Predictable," said Jen. "And here they say it's a new kind of axolotl! I specifically told them it *resembled* an axolotl. We don't even know if they're related. Will no one ever hire a competent science journalist?"

"If they do, point them my way. I've got nothing lined up after I finish my oak borer story. The freelance life is not for the faint of heart," said Kira.

Madison set down her spoon and asked, "What's so bad about that headline?"

Whenever you forgot that the seven-year-old was listening, she reminded you that she was. Jen explained, "It's new to us. But the people who live there have known about it for thousands of years. They have their own name for it: ostolotl."

"So what should it say?" asked Madison.

Jen considered. "How about 'Cave Salamander Discovers Northwestern Research Team'?"

Madison giggled and ate a spoonful of Wheaties. She made a face. "These are gross. I want Froot Loops."

"My house, my cereal," said Jen.

Madison stuck out her tongue.

To Kira, Jen said, "So is this why my phone has been sounding like a Geiger counter at Chernobyl all morning?"

"What's Chernobyl?" asked Madison.

"Awful nuclear meltdown. If you went there, you'd get radiation poisoning and probably grow a second head." Jen made a scary face at her.

"And yes, the story's been making a real splash," said Kira. "The internet loves you."

"Oh, no," said Jen. "The internet loves the ostolotl."

—

It did. The six-inch salamander had enormous round eyes, a mouth like a puppy, fluorescent blue stripes, and fluffy gills sprouting from the sides of the face. There was fan art. There were "uwu ostolotl" memes. By the time *Pseudonecturus ostolotli* was formally described, there was a movie in the works.

"You're a celebrity," said Jen, looking into the tank that housed the lone ostolotl they'd been allowed to collect for the study. "We should charge admission. It would be the end of our funding troubles."

"That *Full Throttle Ostolotl* movie gets funding, but we can't get grant money," said Enrique, Jen's dour, kohl-eyed graduate student.

"What can I say? The world has an insatiable desire for cartoons about motorcycle-riding amphibians," said Jen. "If you could copyright a lifeform, I'd be a millionaire."

"We've got bigger problems than how to monetize our lab animals," said Enrique. "The Mexican envoy called. Ecotourism around the cave is becoming a problem, and they caught two more poachers. Those things are a hot commodity in the exotic pet market."

"People ruin everything," said Jen. "How are poachers even getting into the cave? It's submerged."

"Divers, I guess. Same as us. Worth it at the prices they go for."

"I describe a species, and instantly it's on the brink of extinction."

"That's herpetology," said Enrique. "You have to be masochistic to go into a field where we lose dozens of species every year."

"Yeah, well, I'd rather not be personally responsible for this one."

Enrique shrugged.

Jen said, "It would significantly improve my day if you told me the Illumina sequencing worked."

Enrique shook his head. "The Illumina method is a bust. Its genome is too big. We'll have to use a different method."

"Get on that," said Jen. "Unless we plan to fund this lab on Patreon, we need to get some non-meme-based science done."

———

"Lizard only has one Z," said Madison, sulking in the back seat in leggings and Converse. "How am I supposed to know that? Stupid spelling test."

"I'll help you study," said Jen.

"You're too hard. I'm not smart like you. I want Muddy." The mashup of *mommy* and *daddy* was her name for Kira.

"They're still out researching their oak borer story. They'll be home soon."

"I don't care about their stupid beetle story. I wish we were still at Dad's house. Why'd we have to leave?"

Kira had explained many times, but Madison kept asking. Jen tried to think of how to put it. "Your father … he loved your muddy when they dressed and acted one way. But when they acted a different way, he had a problem with it. You can't love half a person. Kira needs to find someone who accepts the whole of them."

"But what about me? Why doesn't anyone ever think about me?" Madison slammed the door as she got out of the car.

Kids. Jen had never wanted children and had no idea what to do with them, but she'd been shocked by how fast she grew attached to Madison. She would have thrown herself in front of a bus for Kira's kid, but that didn't prevent her from constantly feeling like she was constantly saying or doing the wrong thing.

She made boxed macaroni, the only food Madison would eat when Kira wasn't home, and they ate it at the kitchen table while Madison did her subtraction homework. After a few minutes, she threw her pencil across the table. "I don't want to do this. I want to help with your salamanders."

"Genome sequencing is a bit advanced for a second grader," said Jen. But, seeing the girl's disappointed look, she added, "But there's a way you can help. The ostolotls are in trouble because people want them as pets. So poachers go into the cave and steal them, and soon they could all be gone. You can tell your friends they shouldn't keep ostolotls as pets."

"You have one at work," said Madison.

The kid didn't miss a beat. "That's different. It's a lab animal, not a pet."

"Why are you allowed to keep one in a lab but we can't keep one as a pet?"

"Some animals just don't belong in your house. Can you understand that?"

"Yeah," said Madison, sliding off her chair and heading for her and Kira's room, her ponytail flouncing behind her. "Like I don't belong here."

Jen was surprised how much that hurt.

—

When Kira's short-lived marriage had ended three months ago, they couldn't scrounge up enough money for their own apartment on a freelancer's uneven salary. Jen had been surprised to get a call from her college roommate and even more surprised when Kira asked if she had space for two guests. But it was neither easy nor safe to look for apartments in Kira's position. Of course Jen said yes.

But moving in together had been rockier than any of them had expected. The easy, half-joking flirtation that had seemed so natural when they were in college didn't feel quite right now that they were both adults with careers and independent lives. And Madison's presence complicated everything.

Madison was still in a sulk when Jen dropped her off at school the next morning. It was not an ideal start to Jen's day. Her day did not improve when she pulled into the Northwestern parking lot and found a police car waiting.

Her hope that it was just undergrad mischief dissipated when she found a police officer in her lab, talking to Enrique.

"The ostolotl was collected legally, I swear," she blurted before she thought better of it.

"I'm not here to investigate salamander smuggling," said the officer. He offered her one large hand. "There's been an incident at the YMCA. We need your expertise."

"My expertise? I study amphibians."

"It's hard to explain. You'd better come see it for yourself."

Jen hoped that none of her students saw her get into the back of the police car. At least the officer didn't use the siren. They drove past billboards of motorcycle-riding salamanders and others proclaiming REGAIN YOUR YOUTH WITH ZYKATEL! before arriving at the YMCA. Police cars surrounded it, their lights flashing red and blue.

The officer lifted the barricade tape. Jen felt a twinge of guilt as they passed leg presses and ellipticals she hadn't used in months.

More caution tape blocked off the basement stairs. They passed a couple of forensic scientists wearing blue gloves. Jen's unease increased. On the drive she'd half hoped that the whole thing was an elaborate prank, but that possibility was seeming more and more remote.

The basement was a mess. An inch of standing water covered the floor. The boiler was torn open, and a gaping hole where the drain had been looked straight into the sewer.

In the middle of it all lay the body.

It belonged to a middle-aged man wearing a security guard's uniform. He held a discharged Taser in one hand. His chest was crushed like a soda can. Lacerations covered his face and throat.

Jen stared, fighting down the bile that rose in her throat. "What happened?"

"He was doing the rounds at night. Radioed in to say that he heard some kind of disturbance in the boiler room. When they didn't hear anything more from him, they went to check it out. This is what they found."

"A disturbance," said Jen. "What kind of disturbance?"

The officer hesitated. "Something big moving around. He thought it sounded like an animal … and he heard a sound like a baby fussing."

Jen looked around. It was hard to believe that anything that could do so much damage could make such a delicate sound.

"So what do you think?" asked the officer. "What could have done this? An alligator?"

Jen couldn't take her eyes off the body. "Nothing," she said. "No animal could do this. It had to be people. Someone with a sledgehammer. Why, I don't know."

The officer handed her a small glass vial. "Would people have left this all over everything?"

Jen raised the vial to look at it in the basement's harsh

fluorescent light. It contained a clear, viscous substance. She now realized that the body wasn't just wet—it was covered in the same slime.

"Forensics is studying it. They have no idea what it is. Any insight that your lab could provide would be appreciated." As they left the basement, the officer added, "And until we have some answers, not a word to anyone."

—

At the airport, Kira was looking business chic, in slacks and a buttoned shirt with their hair smoothed back. Madison jumped out of the car and threw her arms around them.

"Hey, Kira. How are the beetles?" asked Jen as Kira threw their suitcase in the back of the car.

"Awful. They're decimating the California woodlands. Nothing seems to stop them." They rubbed their neck. "Ugh, I'm so sore! Traveling was easy when I was twenty. Maybe I should try Zykatel."

"You know that stuff does nothing," said Jen. "It's an iodine supplement your body can't metabolize. An expensive placebo."

"Don't knock placebos," said Kira. "They've been proven to be as effective as drugs in clinical trials."

Madison tugged Kira's arm. "Look at this!" She grinned wide and wiggled her loose tooth with her tongue.

"Gross! Stop doing that!" said Jen.

Madison stuck out her bottom lip. "You spend all day touching slimy things."

"Slime is important to amphibians," said Jen. "It protects them. Their skin is very delicate. Like your eyeball. You know how it feels when you get soap in your eye? That's why we never dump chemicals down the drain." She added, "And it's not freaky like wiggly teeth."

"Can't grow up without losing teeth," said Kira as they buckled Madison's seatbelt. "We can't all stay babies forever like your ostolotls."

"Ostolotls never grow up?" asked Madison curiously.

"Nope," said Kira. "They're babies until the day they die."

"We call it neoteny. They don't produce the thyroid hormone that induces metamorphosis, so unlike other amphibians, they never … " Jen trailed off when she saw that she'd lost Madison's attention.

"I've got a surprise for you, too," said Kira. They handed Madison a trio of movie tickets.

Madison squealed in delight. "*Full Throttle Ostolotl!*"

—

They watched the movie (the motorcycle-riding salamander shocked everyone by winning despite the odds) and sat around afterward in the food court eating nachos.

"That was the best movie ever," said Madison. "Did you like it, Muddy?"

"Yes," said Kira.

"Did you like it, Jen?"

"Yes, but it makes me sad. Whenever a movie like this comes out, everyone wants the animal as a pet. So more poachers are going to steal more of them."

"But if people love them, they'll want to save them," Madison offered.

"People don't always take care of the things they love."

Jen helped herself to another cheese-loaded chip.

Madison was poking around on Kira's phone. Kira cuffed

her lightly on the shoulder. "I take you to a movie, and you spend the whole time on my phone. What's so exciting on YouTube, anyway?"

"Monster attack," said Madison.

"What?" said Jen, leaning over to look at the phone. Had word of the YMCA incident gotten out?

"Yeah, see?" Madison restarted the video. A woman was walking her dog along the Chicago River. A ripple in the water and then, almost too fast to see, a huge dark shape leapt out in a wave of spray, caught the woman by the arm, and dragged her under with a flick of its long, finned tail. The video ended in a blur of motion as the bystander ran to help.

"Awesome," said Madison in an awed whisper.

"Come on, you're too old to fall for that sort of thing," said Kira. "It's obviously fake."

Jen stared at the blurry freeze-frame. A lump formed in her throat. "No, I'm afraid it isn't."

—

The video spiked to a million and a half views in eight hours. Panic set in. People wanted the river dredged. Reports poured in of missing people, dogs, cats—everyone thought the monster was responsible. News of the YMCA incident leaked out. It didn't take the internet long to remember that the Chicago River was connected to the Ship Canal, into which the sewers emptied. People were convinced that the monster might pop out of any toilet in Chicago. And then reports began pouring in from other cities. Some were obvious hoaxes, but some were unnervingly plausible.

"They're calling her Espie," said Enrique. "Because they saw her by River Esplanade Park."

"Why do people always give cryptids cute names? And why are they always female?" Jen dragged everything in her in-box unceremoniously to the trash.

"Don't ask me. Ask the gender studies department. Oh, and the Department of Natural Resources called."

"Tell them I'm not a monster hunter."

"That's not what they called about. It's about the ostolotls. They've had reports of unwanted pets getting flushed down the drain and dumped in the river. They want to know if they could be invasive."

"Endangered *and* invasive. Just my luck," grumbled Jen as she joined Enrique at the lab bench, where he was pipetting ostolotl DNA into vials. "Well, the winter freeze should kill them."

"Here, sure, but they're showing up as pets everywhere. They could be the next thing to overrun the Everglades."

"Just for once, I'd like to not assume the absolute worst will happen," said Jen. "Did you have a chance to analyze that sample I left you?"

"I threw it in the mass spectrometer. It's mostly mucus proteins, but I found something weird: It's loaded with tetrodotoxin. Puffer fish poison. Was that sample from some bad seafood?"

"It's also found in toads and salamanders—including our ostolotl," said Jen. Amphibian poison on an animal big enough to crush a human being. Another impossibility.

The afternoon was all glassware and machinery. The ostolotl in the tank blinked placidly while they worked. He seemed content enough. Jen was glad he couldn't understand how badly she had disrupted his life.

When she checked her phone, she found a text from Kira. "Catch the first flight to Miami. Got a scoop you won't want to miss."

—

"A local angler caught something he didn't expect. Luckily one of his buddies had a rifle," said Kira. "Meet your Espie."

The creature was as long as a pickup truck. A knobby, spade-shaped head with a wide, toothy mouth took up a third of her length. Her thick body was curved into an S shape, ending in a tail with a tapered fin. Her sprawling limbs seemed too short and stubby for her body.

"Want to tell me what it is before I go to press calling it an unidentified creature and get a bunch of conspiracy theorists in my mentions?" asked Kira. They were sporting a James Dean look this time, with tousled hair and a bomber jacket.

"It's a capitosaur," said Jen, unable to believe she was saying those words.

"Some kind of long-lost dinosaur? Madison's going to be so mad she's at her father's house."

"Not a dinosaur. It's an amphibian. These things died out just as dinosaurs were first emerging. It's impossible for it to be here, and yet … " Jen gestured to the creature before her.

"It's not impossible," said Kira. "Scientists thought coelacanths had been extinct for sixty million years. They were wrong about that."

"Hiding in the depths of the ocean is one thing. Two separate individuals hiding in two major cities? No way."

"Three individuals," said Kira.

"What?"

"There's no reason to think that the YMCA incident was the same individual as the one in the Chicago River."

That hadn't occurred to Jen, but she realized Kira was right.

"So what are we looking at?" asked Kira.

"I don't know," Jen admitted. "It can't be genetically engineered—the technology simply doesn't exist. It's not a hoax. It's like it appeared out of nowhere."

"'Animal resembling extinct giant amphibian appears in Miami.'" Kira jotted a note on their phone. "Well, my career is made. How about yours?"

—

"There was a dinosaur, and you didn't let me come? I hate you! I hate you both!" Madison slammed her pencil into the table with graphite-shattering force.

"Capitosaur," Jen corrected.

"Sweetie, I can't bring you along when I travel for work. You'd miss too much school," said Kira. They tried to hug Madison, but the little girl wriggled away.

"That's what you always say. You always have to leave. Everyone does. Just like Jen's going to make us leave!" She stormed in to her and Kira's room and slammed the door. Reopening it a crack, she added, "I lost my tooth, and I didn't even get to show you!"

Silence filled the apartment. Kira gave Jen an apologetic look.

Jen sat on the floor by the bedroom door and said quietly, "Madison. I know the way the three of us came together wasn't the usual way. Sometimes life gives you things you didn't expect, like I didn't expect to find that salamander in that underwater cave. But no matter how it came together, a family is still a family. And I promise you, I would never make you leave."

The door reopened a hair. "Not ever?"

"Not ever."

Madison emerged and wrapped her arms around Jen's waist.

Kira put on the *Full Throttle Ostolotl* Netflix show, and the three of them watched it with a bowl of popcorn sprinkled with cheese powder, Kira's favorite recipe from college.

When Madison was comfortably asleep between them, Kira asked Jen, "Did you mean that? About never making us leave?"

"I wouldn't lie to a kid."

"Oh, man, you could never be a parent. I lie to Madison all the time. I told her a fairy would take her tooth. I said there wasn't any more popcorn when I have two more bags in the back of the pantry." They put a handful of popcorn in their mouth and crunched it.

"Maybe not a parent," said Jen. "How about a fun aunt?"

"Whatever you like. I was never big on labels anyway."

Kira put their head on Jen's shoulder and, even though Madison was asleep, they started the next episode.

"Gah, my leg's asleep," said Kira as the credits rolled. "You'll have to help me get up. When did I get so old? I even tried Zykatel, but it didn't help."

"Of course not. It's specifically formulated so the human body can't absorb it. A dose of eight hundred times your daily value of iodine would kill you otherwise. It just comes out in your pee … "

As Jen spoke, something clicked in her mind.

"You just said 'pee' and then got a look like Moses receiving the commandments," said Kira. "That's a bit weird."

"Kira," asked Jen, "how many people take Zykatel every day?"

"Two-point-eight million. I did a piece on it. God, I hate health reporting."

"That's two-point-two billion doses of iodine every day. Going into sewer systems all over America."

"So?"

"So I know where the capitosaurs are coming from."

———

Amid the panic over Espie the river monster, it wasn't hard to convince Northwestern to close its pool. The pool had to be emptied, refilled with unchlorinated water, and adapted into a giant, murky fish tank with a silty bottom and plants. They stocked it with perch and bluegill.

All for a six-inch salamander.

The ostolotl seemed perfectly happy sitting on the bottom of the shallow end, his gills waving as Jen poured crushed Zykatel tablets into the water. The powder stained the water pink as it dissolved.

She locked the pool doors and whispered, "Good night, little guy."

———

She brought Kira the next day. A good experiment called for a good science journalist. Before she opened the door, Jen handed Kira a tranquilizer rifle she'd acquired from Natural Resources.

"Just in case," she said, not that it would be much help if something did happen. She herself carried a bucket of raw herring.

The muddy water was deceptively still. No ripple of fish.

"'The fishpond, complete with reeds and duckweed, is an incongruous sight amid the diving boards and antiseptic white tiles,'" Kira muttered, swiping their thumb across their phone keyboard. "So what am I here to see? Because you didn't bring me out here just to witness your weird aquaculture experiment."

Jen threw a fish toward the water.

The creature launched himself into the air, breaking the surface with a tremendous splash. Big blunt head. Stubby legs. Rows of teeth.

A capitosaur.

Kira dropped their phone.

"How?" was all they could say.

"He grew up," said Jen. "Ostolotls remain in juvenile form their entire lives. But their DNA still contains the blueprint for their adult form—they simply never reach it. Iodine triggers their thyroid to release the hormone that causes metamorphosis. Humans can't metabolize Zykatel, but apparently amphibians can. It appears ostolotls are capitosaurs in their larval form."

Kira whistled. "Well," they said, "humans had a good run."

—

"Is that one a capitosaur?"

"That's a protoceratops."

"Is that one a capitosaur?"

"That's a maiasaura."

"Is that one a capitosaur?"

"Okay, now I know you're messing with me. That's Sue, the T. rex."

Jen smiled to herself as Madison explored the fossil skeletons, Kira in tow. A day at the Field Museum seemed like an oddly normal activity in a world inhabited by giant predatory amphibians, but Kira said they deserved a reward.

The captive capitosaur, now ensconced at the aquarium for further study, had vaulted Jen and her lab to instant fame in the science world. Kira themself was being bombarded with requests for stories.

"Not another one!" they said as their phone buzzed yet again. They turned it off. "If *The Atlantic* wants me, they can get in touch on Monday."

Jen chuckled. "I bet a week ago you wouldn't have guessed you'd be turning down story requests."

"Yeah, well, there are a lot of things I wouldn't have guessed a week ago," murmured Kira. They laced their slender fingers through Jen's. Today they were wearing blue eyeshadow and a belted mermaid-hem coat, and they smelled faintly of bergamot perfume. Jen leaned her head on their shoulder as they watched Madison read the interpretive signs.

"Eryops," Madison read, sounding the name out carefully. "It's an amphibian! Like a capitosaur!"

"Nice find! Maybe you'll be a herpetologist someday, too," said Kira. To Jen they said, "How many of them are out there, do you think? Ten? A hundred? A thousand?"

"I don't know," Jen admitted. "Pulling Zykatel from the shelves should curb them, but there are a lot of other ways for iodine to get into the water system. We could be looking at a new naturalized species."

Her eyes wandered over a mural of a Permian swamp. Capitosaurs had once stalked through those primeval shallows, the kings of their domain until crocodiles and dimetrodons edged them out. Such mighty beasts forced to shrink and retreat into a submerged cave in Mexico.

Two hundred million years. It was a long time to wait for a drop of iodine.

Separation

Janay Brun

The stillness is scary. No sound or movement comes from her body. I nudge her with my wet nose—a soft touch that we have shared so many times before. A touch between mother and child. I lie down next to her and wait. My stomach growls. It has been hours since I fed. She must be tired from the hunt.

The sun was not yet out. I woke up curled into her warmth. My small movement was enough to direct her watchful eyes in my direction. She blinked. I blinked back. She began to groom me. First my face and then my back and next my ears. The ears tickled the most. I rolled over to rub her tickles away with my small paws. She yawned and got up to stretch. I followed, mimicking her movements. We lengthened our bodies in unison. Our paws mirrored in placement on the ground as our backs formed two parallel, slanted lines. It was now time to move.

We had padded down to the nearest water hole, tucked under a rock ledge surrounded by a canopy of green and shadows. My body had come alive with the moisture. After lapping up the cool liquid, she had lain down and welcomed me to feed. I suckled her warm, sweet milk until I fell asleep.

When I awoke, I had been hidden away in a familiar bush. It was large, with sharp edges on its leaves. I could curl up under its girth and watch our neighbors' movements. Tufts of colors flew between the vegetation. Rabbit would hop by on occasion and give me the evil eye for taking her favorite hiding place. Once a deer browsed close by until a breeze brought the scent of my mother to his nostrils. Then, with a flick of his white tail, he disappeared into the landscape.

I lazily kept an eye open as I waited for my mom's return. I must have fallen asleep again because I jumped with a violent jerk. A loud crack had echoed among the canyon walls.

A strange smell wafted to my hidden place. It became overwhelming in its strangeness and pushed me into the shadows of the waning day. Also, my stomach prompted these movements. It had been hours since I fed—where was she?

I padded down the trail toward the smell. I wasn't sure if I should hide or run toward it. But I was missing my mom and confused why she didn't come to check on me after such a strange sound—where was she?

Raven cawed overhead. She circled high above instead of coming down to visit. Why didn't she want to play—with me chasing her shadow as she circled closer and closer toward the ground, making it larger and easier for me to catch? I continued on our familiar, worn trail until I saw her.

She was lying still. Blood from her latest kill covered her body. She must be tired to not greet me. It must have been a long hunt.

I lie next to her, soaking in the scent of our home— creosote bushes, crystallized dirt, and the crush of grasses. But there is another smell: death. I nudge her again, but she doesn't respond.

I nuzzle deep into her diminishing warmth and begin to feed. As I do, Raven caws right above me, forcing me to look up to see what is wrong. But I am too late. Something rough sweeps me up into its dark depths. I am lifted away from my mother and bounced into the air away from her and my home.

—

I am swaddled against my mother's back. Her heartbeat thuds in unison with mine. She has lulled me to sleep over thousands of miles with soft words and lullabies, so I am startled when she suddenly shouts out, *"Ayuda, ayuda."* I raise my head to peer over her shoulder and see a white truck with green stripes. Men climb out of the truck and respond back to my mom, *"Alto."* She stops and turns her head to whisper into my ear that we are saved.

The men come over to my mom and speak an unusual version of Spanish, but my mom understands. She reaches behind her head and lifts me from her back, tickling me in the process. I giggle as the men come closer.

We are given water and cookies. My mom talks to one man beside the truck as the other stands behind me with his hands on my shoulders—they are heavy.

My mom is gone for a long time. I watch her as I eat my cookies. I chew them slowly, savoring the sweetness of the chocolate and sugar. I sip the water given to me, savoring its wetness and coolness against my throat. I do these things as I watch my mom begin to cry. Her shoulders shudder against her sobs. I drop my cookie and try to run to her, but the heavy hands on my shoulders keep me in place. *"Alto,"* he whispers.

My mom is finally allowed to leave the one man and come back to me. I wait with outstretched arms for her to pick me up and put me on her back to continue our journey. Instead, she grabs my hand, and the man holding me in place lets her walk me to the back of the big truck. The other one, tall and white, opens the back door and motions us inside.

My mom steps into the truck first. It is then that I notice the holes on the bottom of her shoes. Her once-white socks peek through the worn canvas fabric, showing their new muddy color with holes in their cotton that expose the bottom of my mom's feet—bloody and shredded. I follow those damaged feet into the back of the dark truck. It smells of other people's sweat. My mom sits on the edge of the bench to the left. I follow to squeeze next to her on the crowded metal. She lifts me, instead, into her strong arms and places me on her lap.

The doors close shut behind us. My mom places her head in my Hello Kitty sweatshirt and silently begins to cry. A strange voice from the front of the truck whispers, "*Estará bien.*"

We bounce in the truck for a long time. I try to be still so my mom will think that I am okay, but inside I want to run. I want her to open the door so we can jump out and be alone again, just the two of us, walking to our new home. But the door doesn't have a handle, a man whispers; he has already felt for one.

The movement stops. The door opens. We are motioned to jump out into the darkness. Just like we were told to do from the train. A moving train they call *La Bestia*. We were told to jump if we didn't have the money to pay the bribe the machete-clad and masked man had asked for me. My mother had grabbed me tight and jumped. We landed and rolled onto soft grass, unharmed. "*Gracias, Dios,*" she had whispered.

One of the green men extends his arms to help lift me down. I can't move toward him. I stay on my mother's lap. She sits up and swiftly swings me onto her back. I grasp her tight around her neck and slow my breathing so that our hearts beat in unison again.

My mom steps outside, and we are led into a low cement building that is lit up like the *fútbol* stadium that we had passed in Mexico. We had skirted the big cement building, dreaming of the Cokes and candy the others were enjoying. Dreaming of being able to enjoy life again.

My mom and I are first in line. Behind us are two other mothers, three children, and one dad. A new green man shows up and asks us to follow him. He looks like us—brown, short, and squat. We are led into a big room and told to sit on white chairs against a gray wall. The lights hurt my eyes, so I hide them in my mother's black braid. We wait.

Finally, my mom is asked to come talk to a woman in the same green uniform as the men. She has a warm smile and gives me another cookie. I share it with my mom as she answers the woman's questions about our names, ages, and where our home is—was. When we are done, the woman tells my mom that a doctor is going to check us over, but he will do it separately. My mom will go to one room and I, along with the other kids, will go to another. I hold on to my mom tighter as I am still wrapped around her. My mom starts repeating the word *no* while she shakes her head. The repetition of the word is steady and calm, like when I have been caught doing something wrong. The same doctor can see us both, together, she states. The woman, who used to have a warm smile, now looks like a monster as she explains that *la migra*'s policy is to have two separate doctors, one for me, one for her. My mom continues to shake her head *no* as my heart beats faster, out of time with hers. The monster says it has to be done if we want to stay. We want to stay, together. The monster repeats her command.

My mom stands up and follows the monster to a door that leads to a room. She won't open the door until I let go of my mother. My mother whispers in my ear that it will be okay, that I will see her soon. "Maybe the doctor will have a candy for you after he determines you are healthy?"

I can't let go. My mom urges me. If we are to stay in *el norte* I need to let go. I know how much my mom wants to stay. I remember her feet, black and crusty with blood so mine are not. I let go and slide down her back, feeling her heartbeat against mine, once, before my pink tennis shoes hit the stained linoleum floor. My mom turns around to squat so that she can look me in the eyes—chocolate-dipped eyes that I have inherited from her. She tells me she loves me. "*Te amo.*"

"*Te amo,* Mama," I reply. We hug before the door opens. My mom tells me she will see me soon. She is then led away by the monster as another one opens the door and roughly takes my hand to lead me inside.

Behind the door is a cage full of kids like me.

—

Strange creatures come to feed me chunks of foul meat in between bars that hold me in a small space. My cage is outside in a land that looks nothing like my own. Instead of sand-covered hills, there are tall mountains with reflections evenly spaced throughout them. Sometimes they are dark, sometimes light. Shadow creatures move in the mountain. The air is brown. The heat forces the brown down, close to the ground, forcing me to breathe it in. Sometimes it makes me cough.

I'm starting to forget the scents of my home, the scent of my mother. I chew my feet to distract myself. My fur is matted with my own blood now. My mom's dried up a long time ago.

Big animals move faster than Deer all day in front of me. Some will stop and vomit these strange creatures that come and stand in front of me to stare. I stare back. Sometimes they try to get me to come to them with bits of meat that they hold between the bars. I never get up. They took my mom; I will never get up.

—

I lie on the ground, unwilling to move under the shiny blanket in the icebox. The green monsters call my name, and I refuse to get up. I know it will scare them. I scare myself. Another kid tells me that the green monsters beat another kid that did the same thing. I don't care. They took my mom; they can beat me all they want.

The day comes when two monsters come and pick me up. One holds my feet, the other my hands. I'm short, so it is like they are holding hands as they walk me out of the icebox and put me on a bus. They put a metal cuff around my bruised wrist and attach me to a bar in front of my seat. Other children recoil at my scent; I haven't bathed in weeks. I soiled myself the seven days I spent in the icebox. I can smell myself, and I am disgusted. But I don't care about myself—where is my mom? She is what I care about.

—

The loud sounds increase. The strange creature becomes redder with each sound. It smells like the one that had carried me away from my home and my mom. I don't know what it wants. I don't care. It took my mom—where is she?

—

The bus moves. I don't know where we are going, except it isn't to my mom. Another kid has told me we are going to a kid prison so the *gringos* can come view us and take who they want. I want to run down the aisle and through the bug-spattered windshield.

The bus stops after a while so the monsters can go buy us snacks. We are also allowed to go to the bathroom, escorted by one of them. I decide to go because I am making myself sick. I want to clean some of this nightmare off of me, but not too much. If I remain dirty I will never be taken by a *gringo*. I will stay smelly until I find my mom.

—

A long line of small creatures file past me. I can smell their fear; it smells like mine. I watch for a while, and I am about to close my eyes when I smell another creature. It is pungent and forceful, and when the creature walks in front of me, it stops and looks into my eyes.

—

The small cat's eyes are gold and droopy with sadness. The young jaguar looks like he can barely lift his head because his neck is so skinny. I see myself in the cat. I feel my own skinny neck. I walk closer and hold on to the bars of the cage. The jaguar wobbles to his mangy feet and moves closer to the bars. We stand there looking at each other.

Brasita de Fuego

Kipp Wessel

She walked our vermilion flycatcher, in his wicker release basket clasped between her arms, out into the center of the maple-framed field. Winged silver maple seeds nicked our heads and shoulders and whirled into the tall grass. The clouds above us were bruised cumulus.

We formed a semicircle around her, and she set the bird's basket on the grass and knelt. Daphne leaned toward the cage and spoke soft words that carried our way in indecipherable murmurs. And then she reached in with both hands, cupped the bird, and steepled her bare arms above her head. She lifted her fingers, and the small bird, his crimson cap and breast bright in the sun, pulsed a beat in the palm of her hand, cocked his head, and darted through maple limbs, then sky, then gone.

His exit was a blink: a flutter of wings, a zip through the branches and into the ether from where he had appeared four months earlier, the question mark of how and why, his small beating heart and 1,800 feathers forever elusive. Daphne stared in the direction of his dart into sky. A healthy gust shook the rest of the silver maple seeds from their branches and flooded the field, as though the surrounding tree limbs uniformly joined our celebration for this one wayward bird's return.

I walked toward her. Through the spiral of maple seeds, she lowered her gaze and arms. Her purple sundress puckered in the breeze. Tears ran in two straight lines beneath her dark sunglasses and down her cheeks, and she turned to me and asked, "It's impossible for this not to be okay, then, isn't it?"

I opened my mouth, and my heart thudded the bones of my chest, and I couldn't form a single word.

And then she gathered the flycatcher's empty basket in her arms and turned her gaze back up into the sky into which her bird had disappeared. For the longest while, she stood in that place and stared, as though waiting for the answer.

—

It was the single mystery that transfixed the avian nursery that summer—a vermilion flycatcher's migration a thousand miles afield from his range. How he appeared in Ann Arbor in the first place, an aberration of avian biology. Brought to the nursery in a shoebox by a young woman who found the featherless infant in storm-strewn backyard laundry, his downy crown and breast slowly bloomed soft shades of mud and then crimson before our resident ornithologists determined his species, one so rarely seen this far north, central Michigan, that it was deemed "accidental."

"Accidental species," Daphne said. Her mouth shaped a wide grin when she repeated the declaration.

I barely knew Daphne then, had only been introduced to her days before when she trained me at the nursery, herself a repeat volunteer from the previous summer. Dark coffee eyes, pixie haircut, blue suede Doc Martens, southern Louisiana drawl with vowels that glided across the room and consonants that wholly disappeared from the ends of words. She stood out in our avian nursery, in voice and vision, nearly as much as her beloved flycatcher.

In her smiling, gentle way, she taught me how to hold songbirds in the soft of one hand; how to part their beaks with a light press of finger and thumb and insert syringes of protein formula, tipped past the glottis; how to hold crows and rock doves by first wrapping their warm bodies in towels. She taught me how to feed mourning doves with seed tubes, orioles with chunks of fruit, chimney swifts with plunged crickets and mealworms; how to wrap tissue-paper nests. And she enthralled me with lucid stories of her Louisiana home and the pecan trees that lined her lawn and the fierce storms that blew pecans to earth like hail before her grandmother swept the storm-blown nuts into piles and candied them into sweet and sticky pralines for Daphne and her younger brother.

Her colorful stories and the way she leaned in to share them, as though she were reliving the same moments in time, were infectious, as was her exuberance, and I immediately wanted to learn more about her and the distant world she knew. Each second in her company held me in wonder. The world outside her blurred.

When she wasn't near, I mixed insect-omnivore diet and thought of her. I chopped fruit and sifted waxworms from meal, and wondered where she was. And when she was absent, in some other nursery confine or sitting on the stoop with her nose in a book, I found myself feathering the stories she had shared with me previously—images of Daphne as a young woman running cypress swamps in search of crayfish—

Daphne lifting the shelled crustaceans between her fingers from the cold creek beds, crayfish pincers clasping air and rotating like antennae trying to fix a purchase. One by one, she lifted the small animals toward the sun just so she could see their segmented bodies and spiraled veins in closer view. And then she'd set them back into the creek, where they darted and disappeared past her naked feet.

As animated as she was telling those stories—unraveling the invisible life of her childhood swamps and bayous—it was our own vermilion flycatcher that transfixed her full attention that summer. Two nights after the flycatcher was identified, she burst through the nursery door with an avian textbook in hand, parted down the center, her face flushed with excitement over what she had just discovered.

"You need to see this crazy courtship dance this bird does," she said, and she pressed the open book before my face to sequential drawings that showed a male vermilion flycatcher hovered above the trees, his feathers tufted as fat as a hedgehog, followed by a full parachute plunge.

"And do you know what else?" she asked. "Its nickname is *brasita de fuego*. It means *little coal of fire*. Imagine seeing this bird through the forked branches of mesquite trees. In Argentina. Or Mexico. Its bright red crown and breast. A little bird of flame."

Sometimes I wondered if Daphne didn't simply love our flycatcher as much as she did because he made her feel less alone, no longer the only tourist hundreds of miles north of home, no longer the only being who stood out from everyone else in the room—our other accidental species.

—

I had joined the avian nursery, part of the university wildlife rehabilitation center, to help bolster my grades. I was a first-year biology student then. I really wanted to work with mammals, but the volunteer spots in the mammal rescue were all taken. Because they were checking them in by a dozen or so a day, they needed help with songbirds. I signed on to a series of three-hour afternoon shifts and worked them in between classes and studies.

I assumed Daphne was also a student. Maybe she had been. At one time. But it turned out she was more of an intermittent patient at the university hospital, a detail I didn't know until months later.

My nursery supervisor introduced me to her as soon as we completed the tour, and then Daphne initiated my training. She dipped a pair of forceps into a jar of EmerAid-soaked mealworms and plunged the snacks into a cage of seventeen swallows—barn, cliff, and tree swallow fledglings. She swooped the mealworms into each of their open beaks, one at a time, something she termed *the Tao of swallow feeding*.

"Imagine yourself a diving insect," she told me. "Make your final fall from sky interesting."

Daphne taught me everything I needed to care for the nursery fledglings and maturing birds. She guided me with simple instruction, bird by bird—the i.o. diet, the chopped fruit, the seed tubes. She gave me tips for each species and for each individual within the cages—the seventeen personalities of the blue jay in residency; each crow, robin, nuthatch, and vireo. She taught me how to gently wipe the diet from beaks and plumage, how to keep each feathered resident clean, warm, nourished, and hydrated.

But in between our round-the-clock feedings, cage cleanings, and diet prep, I found myself bound to her stories of her faraway Louisiana home, where I imagined Daphne, in pigtails and braces, running past tallow trees and swamp chestnut oak, the cypress and honey locust, the tupelo gum and loblolly pine. They were stories of a place as foreign as Daphne, otherworldly, and I breathed them through the same intrigue I viewed her. Beguiling. Effervescent. Unusual.

Whatever hints she may have scattered of the bipolar disorder she was rumored to be struggling with, the sweeps of emotion I could only later imagine, inverted electrical storms, the splitting of stars across your very own heart, as she was said to have described it, I didn't notice them. I was too caught in her exuberance, her bursting through the doorway, her smiles at each bird she lifted in the palm of her hand, her soft humming as she moved from cage to cage, and the way she leaned into you as she spoke, her words jamming like bumper-locked syllables.

I also didn't mark the days she disappeared, absences I accepted as part of the mystery, the eternal question mark of Daphne—would she be there, or wouldn't she? She was part riddle, part "other"—a foreign being whose family meals comprised names and ingredients that sounded otherworldly to me—green and crawfish okra gumbos, tomato catfish stew, alligator sauce piquante, meals steeped in deep-bellied kettles; in muddy, spicy gravies; ladled into shallow bowls and set beside eggplant dressing and smothered green beans.

Daphne once rattled off the different versions of crayfish her grandmother served: court bouillon, étouffée, bisque, boulettes, and maque choux. It sounded like a menu of meals prepared on the other side of the moon.

Her entire being, accent, and experience were separate from anything I knew. She may as well have had phosphor and neon swimming in her bones, lungs, and veins. Daphne was whole hemispheres—stars and moons apart from anyone I'd met before.

And that's also what made her more real. More present.

When she told me about the places she explored growing up, I could see and feel them—her bayou world of wet, matted vines tangled into the highest reaches of water-leaning trees, the fluttering purr of beetle and cicada wings and chirping pickerel and cricket frogs, the reflected flash of alligator eyes illuminated by shooting stars, and yellow moons emerging through humid, shifting clouds.

And when I was away from the nursery, I found myself daydreaming of Daphne. I thought of the way she tested the flight muscles of chimney swifts—the way she dipped her hand into their cages and plucked single swifts, held them gently, and hoisted them in the air three times before she opened her fingers and let the swifts leap into flight. The birds careened around the room in haphazard pushes against the netting like dizzy acrobats. They looked like little drunken pilots searching for a hidden seam, and Daphne hushed them and whispered, "There, there, there," and plucked them, one by one, from the window screens where they often landed and stared, momentarily, at the wide world spread before them on the other side of the mesh.

The more I learned of her, the more I observed, the more I wondered. What did she look like in her sleep? Did she laugh out loud at movies? What were the shapes of her kneecaps—were they pronounced or submerged into the knee? Were they scarred from careless flights down stairs?

And I imagined pressing soft kisses, as light as dragonfly wings, between her shoulder blades.

Sometimes I found myself staring off into space at the bookstore I worked nights and weekends, a row of customers lined in front of me, my heart lost in thought, my eyelids fallen into the pretty weight of Daphne.

—

I wondered if, over time, I'd find a way to ask her out. Or if I'd at least field whether that hope was a remote possibility. Or maybe the moment would rap its fist across my forehead at just the right time. It would merely happen—without either of us trying. Maybe after I knew her better. Or when she slowed just a beat between the stories of her Louisiana childhood and her undivided wonder about each of our feathered nursery residents. Sometime when the whir of Daphne and the secret life of songbirds lagged just enough velocity to allow more than those two separate worlds the weight and space they consumed.

But if that opening revealed itself those first few weeks of our time together, I missed seeing it. Daphne was too busy moving from bird to bird or from story to story.

"How many variations of bird do you think exist?" Daphne asked me when the two of us crossed paths at the meal prep station one night, and we rinsed syringes and soaped tweezers.

"Between nine and ten thousand," I said. "If it's on a test."

"But how many variations within each variation?" she asked. "Species and subspecies? Anomaly traits and aberrations?"

"At least three," I said. "Until we know better, there's always at least three of everything."

"Do you know how many different hummingbirds exist?" she asked.

"How many?"

"Over three hundred," she said. "That's more than all the kinds of ketchup in the world. Nature invented more kinds of hummingbird than humans can invent of anything."

She blurred logic and wonder into single pulses and dropped them into your lap before you had time to respond, and then she turned the corner and disappeared. She was like a rope tornado, a condensation funnel of sky and wind—like a bioluminescent wave that throbs the shore in luciferin and oxygen and then melts back into sea and salt.

"That's more than three hundred different hummingbird beaks," she said. "More than three hundred different hummingbird tongues. More than three hundred different hummingbird wings and songs and dispositions."

If the courtship of birds was mostly visual, mine and Daphne's was mostly verbal. Her part was verbal; mine was silent observation and wonder. She'd light on a branch, sing a note, and disappear. I rarely noticed her approaching— just the friction of her body moving past and then her voice receding around the bend. She landed in single or double beats, then gone.

Her company was as intermittent as it was enthralling. Some nights I walked my bike back to my dorm. I wanted to expand the breadth of time, the ticking spoke clicks, as I replayed the Daphne moments from my evening in reverse—a bird landing in retrograde motion—her feathers contracting across her undulating wings, her feet tucking back into her torso. I wanted to extend the transition between my shared time in Daphne's company and my separate life where none of her existed.

I walked my bike through puddles, across divots of concrete, over rocks and curbs and flattened sod. I walked my bike with my head lost in the clouds of a young woman I barely knew. My heart beat wet thuds as the stars above me burned and sputtered across the sky.

Daphne and I fell in love with one thing equally and at the exact same time—our new vermilion flycatcher resident. During his first few weeks at the nursery, we took turns giving him extra attention. In between our feeding and cage-cleaning rounds, we stopped by to check on him. When we observed him soundly sleeping, we counted his respirations—the incremental lifts and falls of the miniature metronome of his feathered barrel chest. If his eyes were open, we waved insects in front of his beak, imitating, the best we could, the rhythmic flight of gnats.

Each time his beak parted for water or formula, we felt a swoosh of adrenaline. As his feathers began to fill, as his head lifted with more vigor and steadiness, we crossed our hearts and praised Jesus. That small, red ingot of hope stood out in our nursery amongst all the other chirps and whistles and fluttering wings. He was the only bird housed solo. And he looked at us with wet, blinking eyes, tilted his head at ever-changing angles as if to pose the question—*who are you? And who am I?*

As he gained strength, he gobbled diet and tested his sea legs. He bounced from cage nest to branch and back again. Every once in a while, when we listened for it, his trill call would sing across the nursery room or down the hall. We trained our ears for the squeaky *pisk, pisk* and his chirpy *p—p—p—pik-zee.*

And when we did hear his call, we'd come running to see what he might be trying to tell us. Two wet eyes staring at our expressions. A small feathered head tilting at every isosceles angle.

Pisk, pisk. P—p—p—pik-zee.

Daphne would hold him just a little longer after each feeding. She beamed when she blotted his beak with the damp towel and made sure his nostrils were clear. She'd wait to see him bounce into the cage on his tiny feet before she left him for her next feathered resident. And even then, she'd glance back over her shoulder, in between feedings, in between cages, to see his small crimson body through the slats—to make sure he was still there, chirping.

When he got old enough for solid food, Daphne was thrilled to take him to the flight room, where he got to interact with other amateur aviators—the swifts and swallows—and begin his next stage of wild bird independence.

"Let's give him his first lesson in sallies," she said.

"Sallies?"

"He's an insect eater. He needs to learn to catch his lunch midair. Imagine him sitting on a perch, watching insects, and then he leaps and catches those snacks and flits back to his perch. Those are sallies."

How the hell do you teach a bird sallying? I wondered. I imagined us in flying squirrel costumes, leaping on a trampoline as the swifts and swallows blinked their eyes and stared.

"Where I grew up, we had waders and swoopers," said Daphne. "The waders—the spoonbills and ibis—they just waded the shoreline with their eyes like soup cans. Then they rooted their bills in there and sifted the loot from the muddy current. It's all set it and forget it with those guys. But the swoopers—like kingfishers—those are the guys who taught me the whole aeronautics act of supper. It's all observance and rhythm. They watch every mote and time their leaps."

Daphne caught the attention of a branch of swallows. She moved her tweezer-clasped mealworm through the air in small, tight figure eights, and their heads bobbed in unison like tennis match spectators. She moved the mealworm closer and closer to the gawking swallows, in loops and arcs, and then waved it centimeters from a beak that swiftly plucked the worm and inhaled it in one motion.

"That's how we teach our flycatcher to sally," said Daphne. "He needs to snatch his dinner on the wing."

"This runs counter to everything my parents taught me of digestion," I said.

Daphne handed me the tweezers and jar of mealworms.

"Go," she said. "Teach our bird to fly."

—

I wanted to tell Daphne about my growing interest in her, but you nearly almost always wait for the right moment to express those feelings than create one yourself. And before that elusive moment arrived on its own two feet—Daphne became so focused on the nursery's debate about our vermilion flycatcher's release plans, she seemed less open to social advances or anything else in the time our paths crossed.

She was obsessed with our little coal of fire—transfixed by the nursery's position on whether release or long-term care was the better end goal.

From what I gathered, the avian nursery viewed "accidental" or "vagrant" species as outside our default mission to rehabilitate and return birds to the same neighborhoods that gave them up in the first place. The nursery directors were busy assessing how this one bird might be protected in captivity over release, and Daphne was adamant that release was the only answer.

"You can't keep this bird from the world simply because it's different." She confronted the nursery director one night on our way out the door, after our shift. "Or doesn't belong here. Who makes that call?"

"We're looking into it right now. What the best thing to do is."

The director went on to explain how the nursery's past policy on "spring overshoots" was tied to nimble attempts to try to correct release locations—to split the difference— but this vermilion flycatcher was so far afield of his typical migration, it made even corrected release locations, within reason, challenging. You'd need to drive half the map of the country to set it right.

"So, you'd just keep him, then?" asked Daphne. "In a cage? For the rest of his life?"

"Not in a cage," the director answered. "In a flight room. With the other matured birds who can't return to the wild."

"But those birds aren't released because there's something wrong with them. Physically. The only thing wrong with this bird is its temporary address."

"We're still sorting it out, Daphne. It's complicated. But we'll make the right decisions. Let's just get him healthy and strong first, okay?"

When Daphne and I pushed through the metal nursery doors and out into the night, she took a breath and stared at the clouded moon. She had turned her head, and I couldn't see her expression. I just saw the long stream of breath reach into the sky and her shoulders appear to tremble.

"You okay, there?" I asked.

She let her backpack slide off her shoulder and stood, facing the opposite direction. "It isn't fair," she said.

"They're trying to make the right decision," I said. "I think they're worried about him surviving. If we just let him go here. If he doesn't know his way."

Daphne turned to me. Her face was wet.

"He got here, didn't he? Isn't that enough? For us to let him go here, too?"

I thought of what little I knew—what we had been told, about accidental species—how ornithologists separate the probability of migration fluctuations related to incremental climate and territory changes over those singular aberrations that drive specific birds off their path. Major storms. Incidental magnetic fluctuations. Genetic mutations. The momentary conditions and causal impacts that merely drive singular travelers wayward. Blips on the radar. Temporary insanity. And I thought of the greater, weightier possibilities that signify not an aberration but a decided adaptation of an entire species—the animals that transform their territories, their migrations, their way of life due to changes in their wholesale environment. Food availability. Shelter abundance. Survivable climate and conditions.

The first possibility is the blind taking of a wrong exit. The nodding off before a ringing classroom bell. The second is an entire species shifting its existence.

Our little vermilion flycatcher was so far off his beaten path, the first option seemed more likely. He was at our nursery by error. His zip code five whole digits off.

If true, it begged the question: Should we release the bird at all? In our region? But Daphne wasn't tracing the same logic of the nursery. The trajectory she was following was the bird's right to freedom, his own sense of direction, and all that meant and implied.

"Before we make the decision on release," I said, "shouldn't we first get his adult flycatcher pants on straight? Like, shouldn't we just make sure he can stand on his own two feet?"

Daphne nodded. But she bit her lip and stared into the dark oaks, silent.

"Let's maybe just get him healthy first?" I said.

"Yep," she said.

Daphne bent to her knees then. Her backpack slumped to the concrete landing of the nursery entrance, and her shoulders heaved as she sobbed. It happened in a heartbeat, and I just let her cry, afraid to disturb her, unsure of my role or what to do. She pounded her clenched fists into her backpack several times as a light rain fell our shoulders. A couple of the other nursery volunteers approached the doorway to enter but paused when they realized Daphne was overcome with tears. They backed up and looked to me for direction, as though I had any.

"Daphne," I said. "Are you okay?"

She sobbed and shook her head. I knelt beside her and waited. And then I touched her arm. "Here," I said. "How about a walk?"

I helped her to her feet, lifted her backpack, and clenched it to my chest. Daphne ran the length of her arm beneath her nose, took a deep breath, and then nodded through what was left of her tears.

Drizzle spit the campus concrete, and we walked beneath building eaves and tree limbs to stay dry. The moist air smelled like broken flowers and sky, and I held Daphne's soft hand, the world silent but for the light rain and the sporadic clicking of bicycle spokes, the hiss of tires across wet sidewalk.

Midway across campus, Daphne seemed to calm. She was still quiet, not sharing her thoughts, but her emotions, her breathing, seemed even again, tempered. As we walked, she wiped the drizzle from her forehead with her shoulder, and I found myself stealing glances at her bare kneecaps as we ducked beneath branches: two perfect, round, flat, moon-like disks set midway between her tan thighs and shins.

I had wanted to know what they looked like, and there they were. Now I knew the shape of her tears *and* her knees. Both things known.

"The thing is," Daphne finally said. "All of us adapt. Or we don't. But the important thing is having the chance. We're, all of us, Darwin's finches."

"Darwin's finches?" I asked.

"We're all migratory. We're all accidental species. We're all adapting to this cruddy patch of earth we're bound to."

"We are," I said.

"I know in my heart that little bird deserves his own shot at survival. By his own might. And his own instinct."

I nodded.

"He shouldn't get docked just because he's different," she said. "Or because he showed up in the wrong stupid acre."

When we got to the library, Daphne slowed our pace.

"I think I'm going to do some research," she said. "Look some things up about our flycatcher—"

"You want my help? Or company?"

"No," she said. She turned to me, smiled, and patted my chest. "You've been perfect, but you've got stuff to do, too."

"Not really. I'm happy to—"

"I just need to read more about this accidental species thing. Whatever that means. With birds. And then get my head in a better place."

I told Daphne, then, how she seemed like an accidental species to me. Her girlhood bayou backyard, her annunciated drawl and emotions and the spark in her eyes. I told her how knowing her made me appreciate mystery and the undiscovered. How it made me want to lean into new things and learn them—to see all that's there. It was the closest I came to telling her my feelings, my gathering emotions of fondness, and she responded by tearing up and smiling but then asking me a single question.

"Will you promise me something?" she asked.

"I … anything."

"Promise me we'll release our flycatcher back into the sky."

I wasn't surprised by the question. And I really wanted the same outcome she did. I was right there beside her, rooting for him.

"I hope so," I said. "I think the nursery just wants to make sure that's the right thing for him."

"But that's the right thing for him, don't you think? His wings, that sky?"

I could sense Daphne waiting on my response, willing it, as though it was definitive and held the weight it obviously lacked—except between the two of us—the less significant weight of shared understanding. And hope. The only thing my words offered Daphne was the reassurance she wasn't alone, at least, in her hope.

"We'll make sure that flycatcher is released back into the sky, Daphne. Don't worry."

Daphne stopped and looked me in the eyes. "Promise that?" she asked.

"I promise that." I told her as though the authority had just been telegraphed to me in the same breadth of time I stood before her.

Daphne smiled. She nodded. "Promise me one more thing, then?"

"Okay," I said.

Her eyes teared. "Promise me you'll be there if I'm not."

"If you're not what?"

"There to release him? Into the sky? If I'm not able to be there, promise you'll be there for both of us."

"Of course you'll be there. We'll both be there."

"But if I'm not," she said, "promise me you'll be."

I waited, and Daphne just watched me with her wet eyes.

"I promise, Daphne," I said, and then she smiled, turned, and angled her shoulder against the heavy bronze-and-glass library door and pushed her body past it. When the door swooshed closed and the strike clicked into place, Daphne crossed the incandescent apron of library light and turned up the stairs. Her feet tapped each step until they receded from view. And then I wondered where on Earth Daphne was planning on being in the weeks ahead, if not at the nursery, if not on campus, if not next to me in the open field at the time our little vermilion flycatcher readied his way into the dense air of sky.

—

Four days after our walk across campus, Daphne stopped showing at the nursery. She missed her shifts, left no notice. Single days stretched to weeks, and if the nursery supervisors had word of her whereabouts, they didn't share the news with the rest of us. Her name had been erased from the weekly schedule, with no indication as to why.

Maybe it's impossible to guess at the invisible life that swims into other people's hearts and floods them, the arcing blue currents beneath the skin. I heard the rumors but didn't want to believe them.

Instead, I focused on the task at hand, each songbird I held in my fingers, each beak I parted for i.o. diet and water, each small heart thumping against my palm. When I sat in front of our vermilion flycatcher, I couldn't do anything but think of her—of Daphne. I couldn't do anything but wonder where she was. And whether she was okay.

I didn't have her number, didn't even know where she lived—on campus or off. I knew her purple bicycle, the dented fender, but that's all I knew of her life outside the nursery.

I looked for that bike next to every campus building, each bike rack and chain-link fence, but I didn't see it anywhere. Not her bike. Not Daphne.

I walked the campus library. I walked the stacks, each column of books, each section of card catalog, but I didn't see her pixie haircut anywhere, her coffee eyes, not in any recess of that building or anywhere across campus.

It was as though she had never been there. Just locked solidly and solitarily in my heart and imagination.

And then one night when my chest ached thinking of her, wondering where she went, I walked the long, winding trail along the riverbank and through the arcing pathway of birch, elm, and oak, all the way to the university hospital. I stared up at the blue, phosphorous glow of flickering television sets that bloomed in the windows like candlelight through jack-o'-lantern teeth.

I circled the building. I moved as high as I could on a surrounding rise of hill, as though I might see her through the shrouded glass. I wondered about the tired reach of Daphne's soft heart.

If she was there, I wanted to know behind which window. If she was there, I wanted to reach my hand toward that pane. If she was there, I wanted to tell her I was waiting for her on the other side of the wall, no matter the shape of her heart or head, and that I was on her side. And on her vermilion flycatcher's side, too. Wherever she was, however she was, I wanted her to know I understood what she meant now, how we were, all of us, Darwin's finches. And I wanted to tell her all of it was okay. All of it would someday be okay.

—

I was working at the nursery when Daphne's brother came by to collect some of her things. I could see the resemblance. He was close to her age, the same short height, same dark hair and eyes, the same manner of walking with his chin down and eyes wide open.

She had left a few of her books there, a copy of Salinger's *Franny and Zooey* and several ornithology books. After Daphne disappeared, I had thumbed through them just to see what passages she underlined and to see her inked drawings in the margins—birds and moons and purple-filled stars.

Her brother was on his way out the door, his coat under one arm and Daphne's books in the other, when I approached him from behind.

"Wait," I said. "Just a sec. Your sister Daphne trained me in here."

"Okay," he said. "Hi."

"Hi," I said. "Is she okay?"

Her brother thought a moment and then said, "She will be."

"Where is she?"

"Just resting. Taking care of herself."

"At the hospital here?"

"No," he answered. "She's getting some help from an outpatient clinic a ways from here."

I wanted to ask what clinic and what reason. But I wasn't

sure I would know what to do with the answers, and I wasn't sure it was right to ask.

"Did you drive all the way up here?" I asked. "From Louisiana?"

"Oh?" her brother said. "From where?"

"Louisiana?" I asked again.

"We live in Ann Arbor," he answered. "I'm going to college in Milwaukee in about a month, but right now we're all here in Ann Arbor."

"All of you are?"

"If Daphne told you she grew up in Louisiana, that's just something she says," he told me. "It's probably her favorite version of our life. We visited there once, when we were four and six. But we live on Arbordale."

"By ... Eberwhite?" I asked.

"About a block from it, yeah." Daphne's brother nodded. He smiled a little, seemingly pleased to learn Daphne had continued telling people stories—a trait of hers that made her, also, the Daphne he knew.

"What about her accent?" I asked. "Daphne's accent."

"That's just ... the way she talks sometimes," he said. "Something she sort of invented on her own somewhere. She doesn't mean anything by it. It's sort of like wearing an outfit she just decided to keep on, regardless how it fits."

I wanted to ask him more. I felt about a hundred questions tapping my shoulder. But the foundation beneath each one of them was rapidly morphing, changing and evaporating in the time I stood reaching for them. I felt at a loss of what to ask.

Had I one question alone to pose, to shape into words, it would be to see if she was okay. It wouldn't have anything to do with her imagination or accent or affected idiosyncrasies, but it would instead center hard and fast on the prevailing condition of her being. That's all I really wanted to know. None of the rest of these new and obscure mysteries held any weight against that. My sole question would be to find out if she was going to eventually be okay.

How does a vermilion flycatcher wend one thousand miles off course? Maybe the same way a young woman invents a past life, a wholly imagined and self-learned articulation of consonants and vowels, a human heart of inverted gravity and serotonin. How hard is it for any of us to become lost or reinvented? How easy is it for any of us to land a thousand miles from home, on any given day, in someone else's backyard laundry?

Bird or human, all of us are accidental species. Darwin's finches. Some maybe just a little more than others. And all of us steadying our hope of release.

"Wherever she found it," I said. "Her accent. I miss it. And her imagination. Especially her imagination."

Her brother nodded. "I'll tell her you said hi." He smiled and turned.

"Wait," I said, and I moved toward him and placed my open palm against the door. "Don't go yet. We have a release date. For the birds, I mean. Daphne's birds. And there's this one in particular. Daphne was really—she wanted this one bird released into the sky more than anything. And we're going to do it. The nursery decided. It's like a thousand miles from where it's supposed to be. But we're releasing him. And Daphne should be there."

Her brother smiled, nodded.

"Is there any way we can make that happen?" I asked. "That Daphne could be there? It's next Saturday. At Eberwhite Woods. Near you."

"Let's try," he said. "I'll see what I can do."

"Okay, good," I said. "And when you see her, can you tell her just this one thing, too?"

Her brother tucked Daphne's books back up under his arm and nodded.

"Birds are unstoppable long-range dispersers regardless of what's up against them," I said. "Sometimes over the widest oceans. We don't often give them the credit they deserve. But I read that from an ornithologist. In one of Daphne's own books you hold in your hands."

Her brother smiled.

"Just remind her of that," I said.

—

Some things most don't know about birds:

- An infant crow's eyes are a deeper, softer blue than sky.

- Swifts and swallows drink and bathe on the wing—they gust over lakes and rivers and dip their beaks mid-flight.

- Brown-headed nuthatches often use a small swatch of bark clenched in their bills to pry other pieces of bark in search of larvae, proving the avian use of tools.

- Chimney swifts use their own saliva to cement bowing, cup-shaped nests inside chimneys or hollow trees.

- Hummingbirds can fly as fast as sixty miles per hour.

- Woodpeckers' nostrils are feathered and narrowed to protect them from inhaling sawdust.

- Winter wrens build extra "dummy" nests. The dummy nests are never used, and ornithologists are unclear as to the reason they're built.

Things I didn't know about Daphne:

- Nearly everything.

—

I never saw Daphne again after the late summer afternoon when we released the birds, when she set her vermilion flycatcher back into the sky, Daphne, our own *brasita de fuego* securing the dance of one wayward vermilion flycatcher somewhere, presumably, between Michigan and Mexico. But I never forgot her, never stopped wondering how she was doing, how and where she ended up. I wonder those things still.

I was nineteen years old that broken summer we met. The world was huge. I let its wide sweep, my own fears and inexperience, keep me from reaching across and finding out, separating the Daphne I imagined from the real one floundering and pushing forward in the world. I don't know why I hesitated as much as I did. To know her. To understand her. To show my interest in her. Maybe I tricked myself into believing Daphne would return to campus, to the nursery, and there would be time to bridge the distance between what I imagined and what was true. Or maybe I was too timid then to know the way to asking the right questions or the path to her remarkable heart.

Imagining was easy. It came without trying. Knowing

her, understanding her—I barely had time or access. But I'm not altogether sure I would have known my way there if I had.

Like our wayward flycatcher, it's easy to be drawn to something that stands out like a sore thumb. It's harder to understand it.

But still. All this distance between *there* and *here*, I still wish I could take her soft hand into mine, lean in, kiss those whispers I imagined across her eyes, warm each secret hiding beneath them, and answer the final question she asked me that day in the open, maple-lined field with the wind in her bangs and the helicopter seeds pinging our shoulders. Unsure of a better place between here and sky, I'll use the simple space of this white page to answer her, as if she might somehow find her way to my answer.

Yes, Daphne, to answer your question of all those wandering years ago. Wherever you are, in those cypress bayous or maple seed–scattered fields, with resumed flights of birds above our heads, wherever feathered wings dare open, it's impossible for this not to be okay.

It's impossible for any of this not to be okay.

Ava

Denise Rettew

Ava had invited the animals many times before. She wasn't sure why they'd decided to come today but felt delight in all of her as the pig, the goat, the calf, and the hen broke the dinner table.

First off, before Ava's family lost their bloody minds at the sight of the farm animals on their plates, Ava had grown to seven in an all-American town. What that meant—or what grown-ups meant when they said it—she couldn't figure. To her, the town was a basic town: streets, houses, stores, schools, a hospital, and about thirteen thousand people.

What wasn't basic was the animals. There were more chickens than people. Ava learned young that it wasn't good to say anything bad about the factory farms because "they gave us jobs" and "stupid fucking chickens don't know or feel." *Us* wasn't Ava's family. Her mom and dad both worked as nurses at the hospital. She'd heard it mostly from Becky's parents next door, who didn't work at the factory farms either, but they ate chicken and said they'd enjoy running over the animal rights people with their signs.

Ava'd never told them about her and the animals. They wouldn't believe her, and she thought they wouldn't let her play with Becky if they knew. She'd never told anyone.

—

"Stop asking," Ava's mom said anytime Ava asked her when they could get a pet. "You know Jeremy's allergic to animal dander and bananas." Jeremy was Ava's baby brother.

"They can stay in my room," Ava'd plead. "I promise I will do everything for them. You will be so proud of me for keeping my word and for being responsible."

"Good try," her mom would say, and then she'd leave the room. If they were outside, she'd go inside.

A lot of times Ava considered taking Jeremy in his stroller and leaving him at the Dollar General, four blocks away. A nice, middle-aged cashier named Missy with fuzzy red hair and wrinkles worked there. Ava bet she'd take Jeremy; then she'd be able to get a cow, pig, chicken, goat, horse, sheep, duck, and even consider a dog.

This was all a daytime fantasy. Ava knew she couldn't kidnap her baby brother and give him to a stranger. The imagining gave her something to put over the pain of her longing, like a bandage over a cut that never healed.

—

Ava stopped eating animals when she was five. A lot of people couldn't remember being that age, but she could remember all the way back to two. Those memories didn't have much focus: her wearing nothing but a diaper, her mom holding her and looking at her for some reason, and her dad's old blue car and being in the back in a car seat while he drove around trying to get her to take a nap. That last detail about the nap she'd been told. "Terrible napper," her dad had said, explaining the reason for the daily afternoon drives.

By five, Ava's memories had a clearness to them, as if she'd used her mom's phone and videoed a bunch of good and bad stuff. Her mind, like her mom's phone screen, precisely captured and recalled a moment in her childhood, often coming to her when she didn't even try to remember.

It had always hurt to recall the day Ava'd killed an animal. The blood and inside bits on her small hand. The last seconds of breath, and then none. All the before seconds, too, where she wished more than anything that she could have done something differently.

Seeing the broken table legs and jagged edges of broken plates and her dad's new casserole recipe turned upside down and spilling all over the floor, Ava thought she just might be able to loop the ends of two separate days and tie a knot and never, ever, never question again why.

—

"Change your brother's diaper for me," Ava's mom said a lot.

"Okay," Ava said and picked her brother up, his arms and legs swinging at her.

Ava's mom's whole self looked tired. She'd been this way for months. Her doctor called her a Covid "long-hauler." Besides being tired, all these weird things kept popping up in her body. She'd gotten welts two weeks ago on the back of her left hand. A month ago, her tongue had doubled its size. The bony parts of her knees made her cry, they hurt so much.

For days Ava's mom had to be in bed, and Ava would play

mom to Jeremy. It kind of tickled her to pretend. Once when she took him out back and lifted him into the baby swing, she told him to call her *Mom*. He did and giggled.

Ava's dad cooked now. He'd cooked before sometimes, but now he cooked most days except when they'd do takeout. He came home from work and went right to the kitchen. He made basic food like spaghetti, hot dogs and fries, pizza, or tacos. Ava suspected because he'd made something different today, the animals had noticed.

Ava's mom sat in a living room chair. Her dad had moved it and pulled it up to the dining room table. The hard wood dining chair hurt every part of her body that touched it.

Ava sat next to Jeremy so she could feed him. She could feed herself at three, but he had trouble holding a fork and spoon and liked to use his hands. "Boys are slow learners," Ava's mom said once, only to her. "You'll see," she said, grinning, her smile holding a joke that only she understood but promised Ava would one day.

"What is this?" Ava's mom said as Ava's dad set a casserole dish on the table.

"It's a new recipe," he said. "We need some flair." His blue scrub shirt had food stains on the front.

"It looks delicious," Ava's mom said. She wouldn't eat much. That had popped up a few days ago, and she'd lost five pounds already.

"Ava, say grace," her dad said.

Jeremy tried grabbing his fork that he'd drop, but Ava's reflexes beat him every time. Her hand clamped down on his. He cried out, then she said the grace she always said.

"Thank you, God, for this food, for my mom, dad, and my brother. Please tell the animals it's dinner time. Amen."

"Short and sweet," her mom said with a wink.

And then, after two years of asking them every single day, they came. It was magic. Ava's empty plate became a pig. Her mom's plate a goat. Her dad's a calf. Jeremy's a hen. All real and full-sized, and that broke the table. Ava took a piece of one of the broken table legs as proof. She'd keep it under her pillow, like a baby tooth for the tooth fairy, and make a wish. *Let me keep them. Please, please, please, let them stay.*

Even with all the cuts, dried blood, limps, clipped tails and ears, and the chicken's busted beak, the animals looked beautiful. Ava would bathe them outside in her purple plastic swimming pool. She'd get the peroxide from underneath her mom and dad's bathroom sink and tend to the wounds. She'd mend the pig's broken ear with a few stitches. Put casts on the calf's broken front legs. The goat, too. His back left leg might need to be amputated, with all the pus coming out of his knee and ankle. And, of course, the chicken's broken beak. She'd have to think about that fix.

Ava could always ask the chicken how to fix her beak. Chickens liked helping when they could.

—

At five, during Ava's third week of kindergarten, Hurricane Florence came through, first flooding the southern coast of North Carolina, then inland. All the news covered the trees that had fallen on houses and days and days and inches and inches of rain. Wilmington, a big city an hour away, had gotten water-trapped. They had to fly food and supplies in. Aunt Karen said a helicopter landed in her Harris Teeter parking lot, and army men and women got out and carried bottled water to the entrance.

It took a few days for the reports to show up about the

animals. Ava didn't need a newsperson and a camera to tell her. She'd seen and smelled the dead chickens. The ones who washed a mile from the flooded factory farms to her front yard, dead as doornails. And the ones still half alive, who'd managed to tread water only to be shot or choked or beaten, then thrown into the back of a pickup truck and sold.

The animal activists tried saving a lot, too. They were the ones who told the world about the animals after the storm. Ava had prayed to God for them to do just that. She asked him a lot, too, why the animals had to be hurt.

"Boil," her mom snapped at Ava when she saw her filling a plastic cup with water from the faucet. "There's piss, poop, and bacteria in that."

Ava's mom knew a lot about a lot, so Ava filled a pan with water and boiled it, let it sit to cool, then decided to have a Capri Sun instead.

With school out until the roads and buildings could dry, Ava, two days after the hurricane had left and after twenty-three dead and half-alive chickens washed up on her lawn, got on her bike. Her mom got stuck at the hospital, a twelve-hour shift turned to forty-eight, so Ava promised her dad she'd stay away from the downed powerlines and not get close to the strange tree-truck men who had come into town looking for work.

At the end of her road, she stopped at the stop sign and looked both ways. The only ones out were those tree trucks, electric company trucks, and the pickups grabbing chickens. It was when she looked to the left and saw a man take a bat out of the back of his truck and smash a chicken's head that Ava felt a current, as if all the electrical ones missing from the downed lines had been redirected and raced through her. She screamed at the man, who by then had tossed the chicken into the back of his charcoal-gray truck.

"What's up, girl?" the man said, his voice a soft southern song.

"Stop that," Ava told him.

The man had the bat in one fist, hanging by his side. Ava'd seen him before around town. He wore big brown work boots full of mud and jeans and a green T-shirt. His brown hair cut close to his head made his head look big. That was hard to do with his body so big, too.

"You stay off Highway 15," he said. "It's still four feet under."

Ava thanked him and looked down at the bat.

"They're dying," he said. He took the tip of the bat and poked the closest chicken's side, her wing turned upside down like a wind-up. The chicken tried to cluck, but it came out more like one of Jeremy's burps. "It's mercy," the man said.

Ava had height for five but only weighed forty-two pounds. She couldn't beat him with her body size or smash his head with her bike. It didn't weigh much more than her.

"Get on, strange girl," the man said. "Your staring isn't going to change a thing."

He didn't know Ava's pact with the animals. He didn't know what she'd do to keep it.

Still on her bike, she did a walking U-turn and then put one foot on a pedal, pretending. Her back to the man, she didn't have to look to know where or what. She said sorry to the chicken he was about to bash and for not stepping in so she could try to save all the others.

Instead of pushing her foot on the pedal forward, Ava jumped off her bike, threw it on the road, and ran around to the driver's side of the truck, the door open. She climbed up into the driver's seat and looked at the large lever in between her seat and the passenger's.

"Bitch girl," the man yelled and threw the bat on the road.

Ava got ready to pull the lever into drive, but a chicken flew up and landed on the hood.

"Get," she told the chicken and started to cry.

The wet chicken drooped, then sat, as if a running truck's hood seemed like a good seat.

The man stood next to the driver's door, which Ava hadn't closed, and reached in and slid his arm behind Ava's back and around her side. He pulled her out of the driver's seat and up in the air, and then he dropped her hard. She stumbled and almost fell.

Ava waited. She'd gotten good at being patient.

The man didn't say one word. He picked up his bat, tossed it, and tried to get that last chicken he'd beaten into the back of his truck, too, but the blood and insides were too slippery.

Ava took slow steps away from the driver's door toward the side of the road.

The man got into the truck and looked at the chicken on the hood.

"Get," Ava whispered.

The man put the truck in drive and slowly drove forward with the chicken still on the hood. He got to the end of the block before the chicken slid off the hood, and the truck's brakes came on.

Ava ran to get her bike. She knelt next to the dead chicken and put her small hand on her side and hummed a song from Bible school that she couldn't remember the words to. Then she walked next to her bike instead of riding and told the chickens along the roadside that the man wouldn't be back.

"You can dry off and find a new home," she said to them, her voice still funny-sounding from crying. "You can be free."

One of them clucked.

Ava got on her bike and rode home.

—

"Ava," her dad called out to her from inside the house.

Ava scratched under Benny's snout. He smiled. Pigs did a lot.

"Ava," her dad said again and louder. "Time to go."

"Okay," she hollered back to him, and then to Benny she said, "I will be back in six hours and twelve minutes."

She got up and went to the calf, the goat, and the hen and said the same thing. Her dad had made a nice fenced-in area for the animals in the backyard and built a small barn. Her mom, now that she'd stopped working, liked to come sit outside on a lawn chair. She'd put it right in front of the fence and watch the animals. Ava brought Jeremy out every day, too, and taught him each animal's name and about their personalities. He liked the hen best.

Ava'd never tell the other animals, but the hen was her favorite, too.

"Ava," she said to Ava the hen and ran her hand slowly along the chicken's back. Her palm and spread fingers intermingled with the new patch of white feathers as soft as clouds, and for a few seconds Ava's skinny fingers looked as if they had feathers, too.

Last of the Sasquatch Wilds

James Edward O'Brien

A simple act of sabotage—cut-and-dried compared to the bloodletting misery profiteers have enacted upon the world for centuries.

The oil beneath the Sasquatch Wilds is primo grade. Fossil fuel magnates brand it *sustainable*, despite the fact that the extraction process threatens groundwater supplies and will displace half of the Wilds' indigenous species.

The average citizen doesn't care. Sasquatch exist as abstraction in most people's minds—a myth, if they occupy their thoughts at all. The average person has never seen a forest, let alone set foot in one.

The Federal Department of Unlikely Creature Management booted Sasquatch off the list of verifiable unlikely creatures to render their habitat drillable. Then came a hunting license lottery to boost revenues. People *paying* to do the fossil fuel conglomerate's dirty work. While Bigfoot huggers level their ire at the rednecks with their rifles, the fossil fuel bigwigs fly in under the radar. After the Sasquatch cull, big oil won't have to reroute pipelines around Sasquatch warrens or tiptoe around *where* and *when* they can drill.

Not on my watch. There's a half-mile-long queue of men in jungle camos outside the border of the Sasquatch Wilds. The queue of hunters regards me coldly. I elbow my way to the front of the line. They grumble threats as I reach the row of park rangers that lines the front gate. I flash credentials to the rangers.

"Federal Department of Unlikely Creature *Welfare*, eh?" One of them chuckles. "Thought Colby's bill to kill your funding passed Senate in October."

"It did," I say. "Doesn't take effect until the next fiscal year, though."

The ranger shrugs. The relationship between Unlikely Creature *Management* and Unlikely Creature *Welfare* is tumultuous. Management is a moneymaking arm for the Feds—hunting licenses, leasing land rights to big oil, and the like. Welfare does what was once called "god's work" ... well, as much as any kneecapped federal agency in a godless world can.

"I'm guessing this isn't your first rodeo," says a second ranger. She tinkers with the knobs on a surveillance drone. "You've only got another hour or so of daylight. We open the gates at five a.m. sharp—make sure you've got your safety vest."

I nod toward the drone. "Colby has his way, those things will make flesh-and-bone rangers redundant one of these days."

The ranger rolls her eyes. "You got a helmet? There's no guarantees they won't mistake you for a Sasquatch cub." The thought brings a smile to her face.

"I'll be all right," I say.

"At least through the next fiscal year," she jeers. "I voted Colby, you know." She's what once might've been referred to as a *company man*. "I'm tired of all these Bigfoot huggers crying over monkeys that'd just as soon eat your garbage, skin your cat, and take a dump on your back porch as they would look at you."

I shrug. A bunch of the hunters at the front of the line gripe when they see me slip past the checkpoint.

"Keep it down," the ranger warns them. "He's a Fed." Boos and hisses rise from the crowd. She might as well have painted a target on my back. She knows it, too.

"Keep it up," she warns them again, "and you'll spook all the 'Squatch."

"You armed?" asks the other ranger.

I push right past him.

"Nope," I say.

"Stick to the trails, then," he says.

I make my way down a narrow, foot-worn trail through sparse rows of conifers. Beyond the pines, invasive bamboo grows in dense swaths—a lure for Sasquatch who've acquired a taste for its shoots and sap.

Dawn's early light pierces forest cover in soft, chalky skeins. Through the jigsawed canopy, the skeletal frame of a drilling rig looms on the horizon.

Sasquatch fossils predate man's arrival across the Bering Strait. *We're* the interlopers, not them. Scientific arguments are no use; science is anathema to the Colby administration.

Ethical arguments are equally disdained. Colby's cronies have but one religion: the almighty dollar, its tuneless choir of stock market spikes. The death of the only higher primate species indigenous to North America outside of ourselves means little in the face of potential profit and loss.

The jackalope, the Leni Lenape, the Comanche, the black bear: If there'd been proper graves dug for them all, they'd stretch across the continent.

The twilight woods are quiet as a grave. I continue in the direction of the construction site. I tread lightly. I am a visitor here. We have always been visitors here—and long after we're gone, the imaginary boundaries, dividing lines, and subdivisions we've Etch-A-Sketched across the globe will be forgotten.

I'm almost resentful those Parks dimwits didn't frisk me. If I had known, I'd have been spared the painstaking process of waterproofing, and then finagling, four *magnetov cocktail* detonators down the impossibly narrow spout of my canteen. The magnetovs amp up naturally existing magnetic fields to the point that they crush heavy machinery like origami in an angry fist. I ferret them out of the canteen once I'm out of eyeshot.

Can't Stop Progress had been Colby's campaign slogan. But this razing of the Sasquatch Wilds is *de*volution—the tentacles of a dying industry that's ravaged two-thirds of the world in an attempt to wring its last nickels from the land.

There will be other cranes, other wells, naysayers rally— but there are only so many financial hits a beast weaned on profit can take before it drops. One Bigfoot hugger and four magnetovs don't seem like much in this vast forest. But the Sasquatch Wilds are home to plenty of impossibilities.

The dig site is cordoned off with razor wire: a football field's worth of uprooted trees, bulldozers, cranes—pyramids of stacked pipes. Diesel hammers have already collapsed several Sasquatch warrens in the area. The hunt could push the species to extinction.

I knot a kerchief round my neck. I hike it up to the bridge of my nose. The bolt cutters in my rucksack make quick work of the razor wire. The moment my boots hit the ground, a half-dozen orange eyes rise from the trenches: a murmuration of security drones.

Bladed, winged things flit like rabid hummingbirds. I swing the rucksack weighted with my bolt cutters to fend off the hypodermic prongs that tease out from the ends of the drones' taloned apparatus. Photo lenses affixed to the drones' snouts whir in their sockets as they try to get a bead on my face.

I have dinosaurs to fell, and I'm batting at mosquitoes. I snatch the bolt cutters from my rucksack. I wriggle out of my boots.

A foolhardy gesture, I know—but I want to know these woods as the Sasquatch do—from my bare feet up. If I go down, I will go down beside them, as they unquestionably will should I botch this up.

The cold earth beneath my toes is a gentle reminder that there is no dying with your boots on in the Sasquatch Wilds. I leap for the closest cover—a pyramid of steel a full story high. It's a storybook leap: adrenal, Olympian—but I trip across a low-lying pipe at the pyramid's base.

My ankle gives. My weight comes down. A kneecap *thud* reverberates through the hollow of the massive pipe. So much for stealth.

I fumble through my rucksack for the first magnetov— slender and oblong. I trigger the activation switch just as a spiral fang pierces my palm.

Molten. Paralytic. Pain. My fingers straighten, reflexively. I bumble the magnetov.

The drone wavers. I swat it with my good hand. The spiral stinger staked through my palm anchors the drone. The pain needles through my system. It drops me to both knees, inches from where the magnetov falls in the tilled soil. The magnetov vibrates.

The piles. Once active, magnetovs home in on the highest concentration of base metal within range. They lay dormant until the detonator is engaged. I sweep my bum hand aside. The magnetov darts through the air like a caffeinated jaybird.

It nails the security drone head-on. The magnetov pins the drone against the pile of tubing. The trajectory with which the magnetov hits the drone wrenches the stinger from my palm. What I'd thought had been the worst pain I'd experienced becomes the second worst. I see stars.

I crawl into a pipe hollow. I wriggle toward the far end. The pipe shudders. A theremin tremolo reverberates through it—then another, as if the sky is raining bowling balls.

I hasten toward the tube's far mouth. I choke back fresh air as I reemerge outside, the air abuzz with drones, their drills and pincers competing with the menacing whine of their bladed wings.

A rickety crane towers above, beyond a patch of razed earth. I sink my injured hand into my pack. Fingers won't work: Waves of prickly heat chase throbbing numbness.

I leverage the strap of my bag through my bum arm and then reach in with my functioning hand. I snag magnetov number two. More stars erupt in my peripheries. I'm knock-kneed. I'm less than halfway finished and halfway dead.

I slap the magnetov against the chassis of the crane. I flick the switch. The magnetov anchors to its host. Two more to go. The hunched silhouette of a pump jack looms farther afield. A sparse maze of smaller construction vehicles and SUVs stand between it and me.

I leap. Tumble. Crawl. Copter blades unsettle the air

above me. Another drone descends—I can't hear it over the deafening acoustics that resound from the stacks.

Two on my tail. I dart for the sprawl of vehicles. These things can outpace me, outgun me—outsmart me. But they're machines. Practical, calculated machines, whereas I'm fueled by desperation, trickery—*impossibility*.

I reach an SUV. I slide headfirst, and the drone collides with SUV chassis, its programmatic more concerned with staying fixed on its target than keeping its sweatshop-assembled shell intact.

I claw upturned earth. I drag myself one-handed out from beneath the passenger's side. I'm short of breath. Short of time.

The second drone skates across the hood of the truck. It locks sights on me. I slalom over the front of a pickup truck. Shoulder and dead arm protest as I roll—the bolt cutters in my rucksack bash against my vertebrae. I hit the ground sideways.

Floaters erupt across my line of sight. I draw a deep breath, air like menthol. A floater remains. I can't blink it away.

It's not a floater. It's the second drone. Corkscrew talons sprout from its apparatus; an amber TV eye pivots in its cyclopean lens.

I fumble for my unwieldy bolt cutters. I try to swat the thing back. But it's no mosquito; it's a machine with no regard for its own longevity—or my own.

It moves in, slow and steady. Its talons pirouette in their fixtures like spring-loaded music box ballerinas, deaf and off-tempo to the haunted glissando that resounds from the pipe stack. I scramble to my knees.

I swing. Bolt cutters glance a tertiary propeller blade with a sharp, satisfying *clang*. Sparks. The drone lunges crookedly. It continues to close in. I fumble for the magnetov ignition.

I've only set two. Without the others in place, I'll be the mayo in the midst of a twenty-ton sandwich.

The drone descends. A talon finds my calf muscle. My leg gives. Ice-hot pain riddles hip to toe. I make for the magnetov ignition, good as dead anyway—dead arm, dead leg, dead meat. Life doesn't flash before my eyes as some claim it does.

Even thinking hurts. I hope my end equates to more than another Bigfoot hugger pissing in the wind.

I paw the ignition. *I'll never know—*

A writhing shadow blindsides me.

Death, I think. *A musk of stale urine.*

The shadow fades into predawn gray. The drone's gone, too. I scramble. My lacerated calf throbs in protest.

I look in the shadow's direction, and see it—truly see it. An agile frame of corded muscle and wispy fur hammers the drone into a hundred plastic pieces against the trunk of a knotty pine. Her chest heaves. Her nostrils flare.

She pries exoskeleton remnants apart with feet wide as my chest. *Sasquatch.* I came to stave off their extinction, and here she is staving off mine.

The beast considers me with tired-eyed ambivalence. I play possum. It isn't hard. I'm halfway dead already.

The Sasquatch stands. Pinched nostrils sniff the wind. She howls heavenward. It rattles my ribcage.

Her call lures them down from their roost atop the steel pyramid: *cubs.* A pair—hunched, they pad on feet and knuckles like old-world primates—toddlers unaware of their size and strength, babies who have not yet found balance in the world.

They scurry to their mother and bleat. The twins arch their backs. They waver unsteadily on massive feet. They play-act pose like their mama.

One of the cubs spots me. He drops to his haunches. He charges. My heart thrums like an angry tom. The cub freezes. He flares his nostrils. Bleats. He does a one-eighty and returns to his mama.

I'm trying to save you, I want to explain, myself unsure of what worth our half-hearted brand of salvation might have this far down the road to oblivion. The mother beckons the errant cub to her side.

She harvests the pine cones that have fallen from the coniferous sentinels that ring the site. She digs between the scales of each cone with gentle, ashy fingers and plucks the seeds.

I stand—I move underwater-slow so as not to upset them. They don't flinch. Only the cub who'd charged bothers to look my way—cub body too young for eyes so ancient. The cub chomps on pine seeds. He studies me with restless bemusement.

I clasp my rucksack. Abandon the bolt cutters. I slink around the far end of the truck. Two more magnetovs in the right spot will buy the family time. Weeks. Months, maybe.

I'd like to imagine this would be the conglomerate's last stand, though I doubt it. How big a headache is this last some-hundred acres of Sasquatch Wilds worth to the forces that strip the world bare, down to skeletal dollar signs?

I reach the big pump jack. Seventy-five grand, easy. I affix the third magnetov to the jack's verdigris husk. Seventy-five grand crushed up and cast to the wind like an old newspaper.

I falter. The Sasquatch Wilds waver against a groggy dawn. The steel silhouettes of razing and digging machines shift like slow-drifting clouds. My sleeves, my pant legs, blood-dampened—cold.

"Blood's ... supposed to be hot ... isn't it?" I wheeze.

Bestial, bewildered ears prick up to words that carry neither weight nor meaning around these parts. Churned earth soothes my naked soles. It has a weight, a texture to it that grounds me. I clench my toes in the loam and remember why I'm here. I glimpse my footprint, dwarfed beside those left by the cubs.

These tactile, temporary things don't do much for the pain, but they shake me from the husk of fear tightening around me, if only for a moment.

I run my thumb over the safety on the ignition cuff latched to my dead arm.

The fourth and final magnetov is warm between my fingers. I make for the final target—the pile driver that towers higher than the tallest tree in the Wilds. Air horns pierce the too-quiet dawn—ancillary security drones en route from Unlikely Creature Management HQ. I hear copter blades through the forest. They dice leaves and splinter branches in their trajectory.

I secure the last magnetov in its place: an imperfectly perfect, diamond-shaped perimeter of torrential magnetism poised to go off at the flick of a switch. I hobble off in the direction of the Sasquatch and her cubs. They've gone—faded into the imagination as Sasquatch do.

I stumble across my bolt cutters. I hammer them against the hood of one of the utility vehicles with what strength I have left to frighten away any unseen stragglers.

I make for the tree line. I flick the switch on the magnetov ignition cuff. Earth trembles. A pterodactyl whine punctures my eardrums. The fleet of stoic, unbreakable machines deflate like the chambers of a broken heart.

The Department of Unlikely Creature Management will bury the story. If anyone even cares to notice. It's easy to see why we shun such stories and such places—places where we're forced to meet ourselves again.

I drift, tinnitus in my ears. Shotguns roar in the distance.

I shift to one side and feel the stiletto jab of bones out of place. The wreckage of the rigs and the drills almost look pretty in the stark morning—like a sheaf of love letters from a giant, balled up and crumpled by a thwarted ex.

I notice one of my stupid boots lying on its side in the footprint of one of the decimated vehicles. Boots that traipsed a dozen dwindling woods like this one—foiled twice as many hunts, scaled slaughterhouse fences, shirked security cams.

My boots have taken their last steps. I feel it in my broken bones.

Branches rustle. Twigs snap—a flash of matted fur through foliage. Bleating cubs bound toward me on all fours. They don't worry themselves with what the world was, or what it could be—only what is.

A cautionary roar resounds from the tree line. The pair skids to a halt. We find ourselves shrouded in the fierce silhouette of their mother against moonlight. The cubs' cold, wet muzzles probe my battered sides. Their mother strides toward us. Nostrils flare. Our eyes meet. Drift.

She cradles me in arms forged in downy fur and corded muscle. She steals me away into a world gone unnoticed by the shortsighted eyes of our own.

Everything That Can Go Wrong with a Body

Elisabeth Benjamin

The new chicken killer is a boy. He comes after school and on weekends, quietly. The old chicken killer dropped dead mid-chicken, leaving it to flop maimed with half a neck while blood trickled from the chicken killer's palm where the blade had slipped through his loose dying grip. The old chicken killer always kept his hands clean, wiping them carefully on a series of stained towels so the blood of one chicken would not smudge the clean white neck of the next. Said, Smearing a live chicken with its brother's blood makes it die two deaths, and this sort of reasoning kept us from taking to the old chicken killer. Said, Come here, darlin', to both us and the chickens. Said, Don't worry your pretty little head; this won't hurt a bit.

That last chicken flopped, and the old chicken killer lay dead of a heart attack, his lips flipped back, baring yellow teeth we'd never noticed before, and I wondered if I should finish the job, slip the knife from that dead hand and finish it. I faltered, and no one else noticed, so the chicken flopped with half a neck for an hour upside down in the metal cone. An hour, and then we tossed it in with the bin of heads. A few days later, there was the new chicken killer, sharpening his knife, and we watched those thin boy arms, their perfect musculature, the blue veins of those arms right at the surface contouring thin boy bones, and he was almost a man. But not quite. The new chicken killer kills quietly.

—

We have trouble thinking of things to say to a boy. We are three ladies, slender-handed for reaching into the cavity and pulling out entrails nimbly. Short-fingernailed ladies, though I am tall. We go home to crossword puzzles. We go home to jigsaw puzzles or babies. We go home to let our hair drop crumpled from bandanas, finding a chicken's pink lymph node where we part our hair, remove it to discover one silver strand beneath.

We want to know what he says about us to his friends, if he calls us old, if a sixteen-year-old boy would call us old. We wonder if he plays in a rock band. He wears a black T-shirt that says SLASHER. We wonder if he knows the time and place for anything. We wonder if wondering these things means we are old.

To him we are three old witches, steam rising from our chicken scalder, huddled around our chicken scalder, reaching in and raveling out those long chicken innards, examining them. He probably thinks we read them. Before going in for lunch, we sometimes slide a few dozen hearts into a white bowl. We sauté them with garlic and butter. We eat with our hands. We offer some to the boy, who refuses.

—

Outside the door of our trailer, he kills chickens six by six. He lifts one from the crate, takes it by the feet, lowers it into the metal cone, and carefully threads the head through a small opening at the bottom. This is the part when I turn away, and when I turn back around he has a head in one hand and lays his other on the chicken's thrashing body until it is still. What does he look at? His eyes are fixed on the hills, toward the sea. Just beyond those hills, the sea. And then he gets the next chicken, and when there are six there, one in each cone, blood drained into a trough below, he carries three in each hand to our scalder, carries them by the feet so the wings open white and beautiful, the only moment a chicken is beautiful, upside-down, with a crimson stain for a head and its wings wide and unfolded, like if the boy let go it would fly straight up to the sun. He takes one step through the door of our trailer and drops the headless birds into the steaming water where the feathers are cleaned and loosened. He sharpens his blade. He does this all day.

—

By the perfect speckling of blood on his skin, we can see he does not rub his arms, touch his face, swat at flies. No smears or smudges, his skin is delicately speckled like an egg. He has incredible self-control—whatever's biting his armpit will have to wait. A black fly creeping around his eye. To anyone else, the flies are unbearable, descending in swarms over the bins of blood and parts. The bin of heads with eyes still blinking, beaks slowly opening and closing. Flies crawling in an open beak and out the neck.

I ask the boy if he likes his new job, and he says, Have you ever killed a chicken? I confess that I have never even watched. Three years of this job and I still get dizzy sometimes when my hand's in a chicken still warm with its life. I get stomachaches. The boy raises his eyebrows. A few seconds later he looks at me square, with what might be pity.

So I sit on the steps of the farmhouse for a few minutes and watch him work. As he kills a chicken, my eyes dart off. I train them back. He is steady and stoic as a man, pretending I'm not watching him. He chooses the next bird from the crate, and I lock my eyes on his hands, squint so I can barely see through the curtain of my eyelashes a quick movement, but no, I didn't see anything, just a blur. I try a third time.

One heavy gray cloud passes, and then it is sunny again but also too late. I return to the trailer to probe the flesh of every bird until my fingertips are withered and pink.

—

My hands are not as small as they could be, so I fell into the job of pulling chickens from the plucker and examining them for feathers. I carry pliers in a holster for stubborn tail feathers. I run my fingers over every part of every bird, rubbing the wet yellow down caught under the wings. I squeeze little black ingrown feathers with my fingernails, cut off the feet, and pass the bird to the medium-sized hands that twist out the neck and slice open the cavity, the gut cut. The chicken then slides down a metal counter to the daintiest hands of all that gently slip everything out into a bucket, reserving the heart and liver. Those hands go weeks without puncturing an intestine. They leave livers perfectly intact.

We talk about everyone in town. She's taken up with old

so-and-so. He's bedding old what's-her-name. I swear he tills that field with a mattress spring and a Honda. Sometimes we turn on the radio and are silent.

I often think about the intimacy of killing a creature. I try to decide whose job is the most intimate, and usually I decide mine—the careful examination of each bird's body. Then I think the gutting, reaching inside where it is warm. Then the boy's, the body all hidden in the metal cone but feet poking out the top and a head out the bottom, then no head. I can't figure out how the degree of violence relates to the depth of intimacy.

And sometimes the thought enters my head and turns over and over, all the things that can go wrong with a body. All the bruises and fat bands and fluids and discolorations. All the broken wings and toes, how easy it is to snap a toe, to skin an elbow, the liver spots, the pneumonia, all the green misshapen things that can happen to a body. The little five-pound chicken embodies all the world's deformities and maladies. If the thought comes to me, it will not leave for the rest of the day. If the thought comes, I will prod at my own body, run my hands up leg and arm bones, searching for abnormalities, and all I've done is agitate black fly bites into itching. My self is whole, bendable, twice the age of the boy who I imagine does not yet regard himself with dread, does not yet expect to fall apart.

—

We are quiet, imagining anyplace but here, and suddenly the chicken killer is chasing a loose chicken through our trailer. I see the boy left in him. He is smiling, crouching, creeping up on the chicken where it trembles under the hand-

241

washing sink. He reaches slowly under and grabs it. It flaps. He carefully folds down its wings, pulls it close to his chest the way other boys hug a football, slightly to one side, and I see his fingers moving secretly within the white feathers. He is caressing it before he flips it, dangles it from its feet, to swiftly slice the neck. There are dignities chickens are rarely afforded.

I look outside. White feathers rise pristine from the thrashing, lit and aloft for a moment before settling in the dark woods behind him.

—

Day-old chicks arrive through the mail, fifty to a box. Every chick has to be taught to drink, its head plunged into the water dish and held there until it swallows. Sometimes we have to teach them twice, the slow learners, so the brooder does not become for them a desert. The topic of conversation is always Why Do They Have to Grow? In three weeks they're moved to the pasture, maybe eaten by weasels or owls. In eight weeks we will hook their yellow legs and drag them squawking into old lobster pots where they will ride through the fields in the pickup truck to our processing trailer. The boy will cut off their heads with the knife he sharpens meticulously. If he came on a day when we tenderly teach each chicken to drink, when we sweeten their water with molasses and apple cider vinegar, would he still think we are three witches?

—

He kills every bird by afternoon, and we take a late lunch at the long farmhouse table. It is astounding how much food he eats. He washes his arms in the kitchen sink, but his face and neck are still speckled with blood. I thought he was freckled the first week. He takes off his glasses and holds them up to the light like an old man, rubs them on the sleeve of his shirt. Then he tucks in and eats at least three sandwiches, plus anything we offer him from our own lunches. We want to endear him to us with food, want him to tell us something. Anything. He wolfs down our offerings in silence and then puts his head down on his arms and sleeps until one of us taps his shoulder.

After lunch we return to the trailer and cut the chickens up and package them. I stay late to bag the backs and hearts and livers. He walks in one night, still waiting for his mother to pick him up, and sits on the stool beside me. He watches, listens, as I crack the backs and twist them to fit in the bags. Backs, I say dumbly. Backs? How do you talk to a boy?

Backs, he says. Backs. Then he laughs a little through his nose.

Backs, I say again quietly.

Backs, he says, and we are quiet after that until his mother pulls up outside the trailer and honks. If he had stayed another moment, I'd have offered him a wishbone.

—

Something I do when the tide is going out: take the bin of chicken heads, hundreds of chicken heads, down to the sea instead of to the compost and stand up on the brown rocks jutting out over the water and let those heads tumble into the waves. They spread and bob away. They are picked up by gulls or pulled under by seals. I watch a hundred white tufts floating, stars on the water, and in a few moments they are all gone.

—

If there is a chicken too small for the cone, one that would slip right through the neck hole, a sick one that should go as long as we're in the business of chicken killing, the boy takes it to the chopping block, slips its neck between two nails, and chops. He releases the body, which floats upward—this awkward creature, suddenly weightless, seems to hover a few inches above ground, spinning quick circles like an untied balloon just released. He watches a moment, in awe perhaps as I am, and then gently sets his boot down on a wing so it flops, confined like we're used to. He says, You done? and it gives one last kick. There is a thin spiral of blood on the dirt ground.

He looks up at me and says, You didn't watch, did you?

—

All the spots and rashes. Gizzards packed hard with sharp objects, a sack of liquid around an organ, everything brittle, trembling, folded over. Voice cords work if you press the body correctly, or if you slam it.

We know a heart can blister. The blistered heart is studied then discarded.

—

His green rubber boots are empty, positioned pigeon-toed by the door, and I tell myself that not everything is a body. Again, it is late. He's in beat-up sneakers, sitting quietly on a stool beside me, waiting for his mother. I wonder if she worries about him, and I want to rest my hand on the back of his smooth neck, the young skin not yet argyled with creases. I want to cup his chin. He picks at dirt under his nails, and the fluorescent light in the trailer tinges his tan skin an unpleasant yellow, and I wonder how hideous I must look. He sits up straight and looks out the open door, into the dark. A clucking.

He says, I lost one today, didn't tell anyone. Didn't feel like chasing it through the woods.

A clucking. The chicken is in the doorway, greenish from the lights. She pecks at the metal doorframe. We watch as she hops into the trailer and picks delicately through some feathers under the plucker. The boy takes his knife from the shelf and with his other hand gently lifts me up by my elbow. Somehow he has already learned how to touch a woman's elbow. I follow him outside, watch him scoop up the chicken, sluggish from darkness. He laces her head through the hole and takes my hand, and together we have the knife, and he is confident I think for the first time in his life as he tightens his grip. I try to pull away: He lays two fingers on my wrist as if to silence a bell.

Once as a girl, I asked my mother how to tell when the chicken's done baking, and she said you know it's done when you can shake hands with it. I am no longer interested in shaking a chicken's hand. I think I will tell him this when it's over.

Contributors

Elisabeth Benjamin lives in rural Maine and works with plants. She has a chapbook, *The Houses*, published by The Catenary Press.

Setter Brindle Birch is the pen name of a debut fiction author who shares her home with three cats.

J. Bowers has published fiction in national journals, including *StoryQuarterly*, *The Indiana Review*, and *Guesthouse*. A three-time Pushcart Prize nominee, Bowers won *The Laurel Review*'s 2014 Midwest Short Fiction Prize and the 2016 *Winter Anthology* Prize. She is an assistant professor of English at Maryville University in St. Louis, Missouri.

Janay Brun relates better to an outside world devoid of humans rather than an inside one full of them. At present she roams the saguaro-studded mountains and cottonwood arroyos of southern Arizona. She is the author of *Cloak & Jaguar: Following a Cat from Desert to Courtroom*.

JoeAnn Hart is the author of the crime memoir *Stamford '76: A True Story of Murder, Corruption, Race, and Feminism in the*

1970s (University of Iowa Press, 2019). Her novels are *Float* (Ashland Creek Press), a dark comedy about plastics in the ocean, and *Addled* (Little, Brown), a social satire.

Gwen C. Katz is an author, artist, game designer, and former mad scientist who lives in Pasadena, California, with her husband and assorted chickens and cats (but currently no salamanders). Her first novel, *Among the Red Stars*, is about Russia's all-female bomber regiment known as the Night Witches.

Diane Lefer is delighted to appear in another ACP anthology. Animals often figure in her novels. *Confessions of a Carnivore* was inspired by her relationship with a baboon at the LA Zoo. In *Out of Place*, scientists become suspect after 9/11 while characters include rattlesnakes, bears, one good dog, and many cats.

Charlene Logan's work has been published in *West Marin Review, About Place Journal, Witness Magazine, Blackbird, Pembroke Magazine*, and other magazines and journals. She received a writing fellowship from MacDowell and earned an MFA in playwriting from UC Davis. She is a volunteer with NorCal Collie Rescue.

Nadja Lubiw-Hazard is a Toronto-based writer and veterinarian. She is the author of the novel *The Nap-Away Motel*; her short stories have been published in *Understorey, Room, Canthius, The Dalhousie Review, Fiddlehead, The New Quarterly*, and more. Nadja is a lifelong animal lover and longtime vegan. (www.nmlhazard.com)

Marilyn Moriarty is a professor of English and creative writing at Hollins University in Roanoke, Virginia. She is the author of the textbook *Writing Science through Critical Thinking* and the creative nonfiction book *Moses Unchained*. She has won prizes for her writing, and her essays and short stories have been published in a number of literary magazines.

James Edward O'Brien hails from Bloomfield, New Jersey. Jim's short fiction has appeared in numerous anthologies and speculative fiction magazines, both online and in print, as well as on the *StarShipSofa* and *Tales to Terrify* podcasts. He currently resides in Queens, New York, with his wife and three rescue dogs.

Helia S. Rethmann grew up in Germany. Her fiction has appeared in *River and South, Breakwater Review*, and others, as well as in anthologies published by Pure Slush, Between the Lines, and Two Sisters. Helia lives on a farm near Nashville, Tennessee, with her wife and too many animals.

Denise Rettew studied creative writing at the University of North Carolina Wilmington and has been teaching yoga since 2003. She leans on these two practices for inspiration, understanding, and equanimity. Denise lives in North Carolina near the ocean, where, after twenty years in the area, she is finally breaking away from everyday life and getting her feet on the sand.

Ingrid L. Taylor is an award-winning poet, writer, and veterinarian whose work has appeared in the *Southwest Review; FERAL: A Journal of Poetry and Art; Horse Egg Literary*; and others. She's received support from Playa, the Horror Writers

Association, and Gemini Ink, and she received her MFA from Pacific University.

Jacquie Vervain holds a BA in English literature with a minor in classical studies, an MEd in secondary education, and an MFA in fiction. She writes dark fantastical mysteries and runs The Mad Girl's Guide to Animal Liberation, a website designed to connect teen girls with the fight for animal rights.

Kipp Wessel loves animals, wilderness, and writing. His debut novel, *First, You Swallow the Moon*, is about heartbreak and grizzly bears. He earned a fiction fellowship and his MFA from the University of Montana. He's taught fiction writing there, at the Loft Literary Center, and elsewhere. He lives in Minnesota.

Acknowledgments

"The Art of Dying" by Nadja Lubiw-Hazard was originally published in Issue 150 of *The New Quarterly*.

"Survival Skills" by Diane Lefer first appeared in *Stonecrop Review*, Issue 4: Fauna.

"Flying Home" by JoeAnn Hart was originally published in the Summer 2021 issue of *The Stonecoast Review*.

"One Trick Pony" by J. Bowers was originally published in Issue 17.2 of *Big Muddy: A Journal of the Mississippi River Valley*.

"The Ass of Otranto" by Marilyn Moriarty was originally published in the Spring 2019 issue of *J Journal*.

"The Curious Case of the Cave Salamander" by Gwen C. Katz originally appeared in *Utopia Science Fiction* in February 2021.

"Everything That Can Go Wrong with a Body" by Elisabeth Benjamin first appeared in Issue 21 of *Meridian*.

About the Cover

Winky is a Cornish Cross hen rescued from kaporot, a ritual slaughter performed by a very small group of Orthodox Jews. She was rescued by Tikkun Olam Farm Sanctuary in 2019 when she was six weeks old; one of her eyes had been injured and could not be saved.

Winky lives at the Tikkun Olam sanctuary, where she will spend the rest of her life among other rescued animals and loving staff and volunteers. Tikkun Olam, which means "repair the world" in Hebrew, is a sanctuary in Southern Oregon that rescues and provides forever homes to abused, abandoned, neglected, and unwanted farm animals including chickens, goats, sheep, cows, and pigs. Visit TOFS at https://www.facebook.com/tofsanctuary.

Ashland Creek Press is a vegan-owned, independent publisher of books for a better planet. Our mission is to publish a range of books that foster an appreciation for worlds outside our own, for nature and the animal kingdom, for the creative process, and for the ways in which we all connect. To keep up-to-date on new and forthcoming works, subscribe to our free newsletter by visiting www.AshlandCreekPress.com.

CPSIA information can be obtained
at www.ICGtesting.com
Printed in the USA
BVHW061921060422
633047BV00003B/18